SCHOOL FOR SCANDAL

Three stories: In *School For Scandal*, Lucy Lockley, *The Bugle*'s chief reporter, suspects the local school headmaster of being on the fiddle — then discovers something far more scandalous. Meanwhile, in *Making A Difference*, new Police Community Support Officer Shelley Lansdown normally deals with missing items — but finds herself investigating the disappearance of a family. And in *Closing Time*, DC Myra McAllister attempts to unravel a murder committed in 1962 — and appears to step back in time . . .

GERALDINE RYAN

SCHOOL FOR SCANDAL

Complete and Unabridged

LINFORD
Leicester

First published in Great Britain

First Linford Edition
published 2013

British Library CIP Data

Ryan, Geraldine, *1951* –
    School for scandal. - -
    (Linford mystery library)
    1. Detective and mystery stories, English.
    2. Large type books.
    I. Title II. Series
    823.9′2–dc23

    ISBN 978–1–4448–1510–8

Published by
F. A. Thorpe (Publishing)
Anstey, Leicestershire

Set by Words & Graphics Ltd.
Anstey, Leicestershire
Printed and bound in Great Britain by
T. J. International Ltd., Padstow, Cornwall

This book is printed on acid-free paper

School for Scandal

1

'Aren't you going to open it, then?' School secretary Mylene Kay, neat and fragrant in her navy suit and high heels, pushed the envelope towards Bron with a red talon. Had she always been this stylish? Bron wondered. Perhaps she had and Bron, more interested in what people had on their plates than on their backs as a rule, just hadn't noticed.

Right now, Bron was in the middle of attempting to create a pasta dish that was not only nutritious, tasty and colourful and cost no more than seventy pence per portion, but that would also pass muster with Mr Staggs, the school principal.

She cast an envious glance towards Mylene's trim form. In the dim and distant past, she, too, had possessed a figure like Mylene's, but that was before her passion for cooking had taken over her life. The inches hadn't so much crept on over the years, she mused, as advanced at full tilt.

'You open it, Mylene,' she said. 'I can see you're dying to.'

'Well, it's not every day you get a letter from the BBC,' Mylene said. She let out a squeal. 'No way! I don't believe it!'

Mylene's shriek brought Bron's co-workers, Sandra and Annette, running. Weeping over onions and grumbling about the amount of potatoes still left to peel, they needed no encouragement to down tools. The two women crowded round her, demanding to know what was going on.

'You've only been nominated for a food award!'

Bron snatched the letter from Mylene. 'Give me that!' she yelled.

'Read it out, Bron,' Sandra urged.

'Give me a minute to put my specs on! Right, here we go. *Dear Mrs Wright.*' Bron read calmly at first, then with mounting excitement. '*The BBC is delighted to inform you that you and your team of dinner ladies at Poplar Green Independent School have been* nominated for an award in the category of *Best School Grub*, as part of the popular TV series Home Cooking's celebration of British cooking. The winners will be announced in September at a special dinner, hosted by children's TV presenter Lily Hopper, and the award to the winner in your category will be presented by none other than Home Cooking's resident chef, Kriss Crossley.'

'You're having us on!'

'Let me have a look!'

'Kriss Crossley! I'd rather have that Jean-Christophe Novelli.'

'Give me Gordon Ramsay any day.'

Everyone was suddenly talking at once. No one heard the rest of the letter, all small-print stuff about judges' visits, which they would be notified about at a later date. No one heard the school caretaker, Len Blears, make his usual coffee-break entrance, either. Which must have been a first, considering the cluster of jangling keys he wore fastened to his belt that could usually be heard miles away.

It was down to Mylene to bring him up to speed with events, since Bron seemed to have lost the power of speech, and Annette and Sandra had moved on from comparing the sex appeal of various celebrity chefs, and were now busy discussing what to wear on the night and whether they'd be allowed to take their partners as plus-ones. Not that Sandra was all that keen on that idea, just in case Jean-Christophe decided to put in an appearance after all. In the end, Len made his own coffee, and one for the girls, too, while he was at it. Though, as he said, a magnum of champagne would have been more the ticket.

'Who on earth would nominate us?' Bron, still dazed, hugged her steaming mug in both hands.

'The kids, it says, if you read it properly,' Mylene said.

'And it's not us,' Sandra said generously. 'It's really you, Bron. Your inspiration and leadership.'

Annette sniggered. 'Is that what you're going to tell the judges?' she said.

Sandra shot her a look. 'Well, it's true,

isn't it? The only veg you could identify was a frozen pea till Bron came along. And that was only if the packet was next to it to give you a clue.'

Annette blushed.

'She's right,' Len said. 'All these innovations have been Bron's idea and Bron's idea only. Whatever nonsense the Principal's putting about.'

Bron wriggled uncomfortably, kicking herself for having let slip to Len, in a moment of frustration, her real feelings about Staggs. Len was only sticking up for her, but she didn't want it getting back to Staggs, through Mylene, that she resented the way the Principal had suddenly started to take rather too great an interest in what was going on in the school kitchen.

'Len,' she muttered. 'Please.'

'Well,' he said. 'I'm only saying. Buying local produce, getting the kids involved in growing their own veg, setting up the children's tasting panel to test new recipes. It was all down to you.'

'But I couldn't have done it on my own,' Bron said modestly.

'It's not the Head's intention to steal Bron's glory, Len.' Mylene's ears had pricked up at the mention of Staggs' name and she seemed determined to defend him. 'But obviously, Bron being nominated like this — well, it's a real coup for the school. Of course he'll want to be involved.'

The atmosphere was growing tense. Bron hoped with all her heart that Len might show a bit more tact when he next opened his mouth, bearing in mind that Martin Staggs' PA was in the room. But Len and tact were not even on nodding terms, so she didn't hold out much hope.

'Oh, he'll be all over it like a rash as soon as he finds out,' he said, surpassing himself. 'You mark my words. Before you know it, he'll be going up to collect the award himself.'

Sandra and Annette giggled. Mylene, clearly offended on her boss's behalf, muttered her excuses, saying she had some phone calls to make. Bron quelled a strong urge to crack Len on the back of the head with the nearest pan. It was as clear as day to everyone but him that

Mylene's loyalties towards Staggs were as strong as Len's towards her.

Len, like most men, in Bron's experience, was incapable of seeing further than the end of his nose. At least Sandra and Annette had had the sense to keep their opinions of Staggs to themselves. But that was more likely to be down to the fact that throughout Len's tirade they'd been too busy on their mobiles, informing everyone they knew about the nomination, and had simply failed to hear him.

'We haven't actually won it yet, Len,' Bron reminded him, to Mylene's stiff, retreating back. 'And at this rate we don't deserve to. There's a mound of spuds still to be peeled and cheese sauces don't make themselves.'

'Not any more,' Sandra agreed, getting off her phone at last. 'Not with you in charge, Bron. Unless we can find a tin of that powder we used to use lurking at the back of the cupboard.'

'In your dreams, Sandra,' Bron said, with a grimace. 'No cheating in this kitchen.'

'Unless it's on the diet,' everyone

9

chimed in, dipping into the biscuit tin, just like they usually did at this time of the day.

★ ★ ★

Bron still hadn't come down to earth once lunch had been served and everything had been cleared up and put away. She decided to pay a visit to see Terri, her daughter, on the way home. If she was quick, they'd have half an hour before Terri had to leave to pick little Emma up from school. Terri would be thrilled for her, she was sure.

But Terri's face was glum as she opened the door and she barely acknowledged Bron's news. Not even the bit about Lily Hopper or Kriss Crossley. There were far too many cookery programmes on TV these days, if you asked her.

'Have I come at a bad time?'

Terri hadn't even asked her to take her coat off. She did, anyway.

'Read that.' Terri thrust a sheet of paper at Bron. 'Then tell me what you think.'

Bron ran her eyes down the page. It was a letter from the local education authority, regretting to inform Terri that, unfortunately, since her daughter had failed the entrance test for admission to the school of her choice, Poplar Green Independent School, she'd been offered a place at Stramley High, her second choice, where they were confident Emma would be happy.

'Oh, dear, what a shame,' Bron said. 'Is she disappointed?'

'No, *she's* fine about it. Stramley's where her friends are going.'

'Well, that's all right then, isn't it?'

'No, it's not all right. There was no way she did badly in that test. Even the teacher couldn't believe she'd failed. She's one of the brightest kids in her year.'

Emma was bright, there was no denying it. But Terri could be very biased when it came to Emma. She'd been just as furious that time Emma had lost out on the part of Mary in the nativity play to Consuela De Souza, ending up instead with the part of Fourth Shepherd, who only had one line.

'Maybe her nerves got the better of her,' Bron said, hoping her words might offer some comfort.

Terri gave a snort. 'Emma's got nerves of steel, Mum, and you know it.'

'Or perhaps she simply got overwhelmed by it all. Some kids are just no good at tests. You weren't,' she reminded Terri.

Terri glared at her. 'That Staggs makes his own rules, if you ask me,' she said. '*He's* got in — little Ben Fielding. 'Course, his dad's a local councillor. And what about your mate, Mylene? Ask *her* next time you see her which school her Jane'll be going to in September. It won't be Stramley flamin' Community College. And Jane only got a Level 2 in the last SATS test. I know that for a fact.'

Terri was getting herself more and more agitated. She'd say anything when she was in this state, Bron knew.

'You could fix this for us, Mum,' she went on. 'You work there. You're the school cook. Up for an award! A word in his ear and this decision could be reversed in no time.'

Bron was shocked. Did Terri really think that was the way to get what you wanted? To 'have a word' in the right ear? And what about the child who would then lose their place because Terri had used an unfair advantage? she asked.

'I don't care about anyone else's kids,' Terri said. 'Just mine.'

Bron's heart sank. In her mind, this was the trouble with society these days. Everyone putting themselves first and not giving a fig about other people.

'It wouldn't make me any different from that Mylene, would it?' Terri said defensively, noting her mother's horrified expression. 'Or Ben Fielding's dad. Or any of those other families who've somehow managed to bend the rules to get their kids a place.'

'Now, Terri. You need proof before you go round accusing people.' Her tone was placatory, but it cut no ice with Terri.

'Ten minutes in the playground at the end of the school day will get me all the proof I need,' she said, before adding, after a horrified glance at her watch, 'which is where I should be in about five minutes, Mum. So unless you want to come with me to pick up Emma, you'll have to excuse me if I throw you out.'

Typical, Bron thought as she got into her old car and drove the rest of the short way home. She'd gone round to Terri's full of excitement at her news, hoping for a bit of company to share it with. But all she felt now was deflated, thanks to Terri's insinuations about Staggs and his dodgy dealings.

She didn't like Staggs, she'd made no bones about it to Len. Staggs was a meddler, always wanting the glory whenever anything good happened at the school, and always ready to shift the blame on to some other poor so-and-so whenever anything went wrong.

Last year, when he'd first arrived, she'd gone to him as catering manager, full of ideas about how to make Poplar Green more self-reliant instead of doing what it had always done, which was to hand over its meagre budget to a third-rate supplier who ripped them off financially into the bargain. But Staggs had pooh-poohed all her suggestions. When she explained that if they grew their own vegetables they could ensure the freshness of the produce, he was unimpressed. Similarly, when she suggested that if they went in for locally reared meat it would go a long way to reassuring parents anxious about quality, he hardly blinked.

And as for her idea of inviting a tasting panel, made up of children, to meet every month and offer their opinions on new recipes, well, you'd think she'd suggested it was high time the lunatics took over the asylum. As far as Martin Staggs was concerned, what the kids put in their mouths was of little consequence. The only thing that really mattered was exam results.

Quite what had changed his mind she still wasn't sure. Maybe it was the trickle of letters in the local paper, praising the school for its innovative approach to feeding its pupils. Within days, what had originally been Bron's culinary innovations became Staggs'. Which was fine by Bron. She'd never been one for the limelight and was always happiest when she was tucked away in the corner of her kitchen, mixing and stirring, and dreaming up new ideas.

But since Staggs decided to become more hands-on, her comfortable world had been turned upside down. These days, he invited himself to taste-ins. He felt he should cast his eyes over the menus at the beginning of each week. He'd even turn up occasionally at the allotment behind the kitchen, in those ludicrous green wellies of his, often with a prospective parent or two in tow, whom he was clearly out to impress. It drove her mad!

But for all that, she'd never questioned his honesty. She didn't know anything about the ability of the local councillor's son, but she had to admit it had been a bit of a surprise that little Jane — who Mylene herself had admitted was behind with her sums and reading — had managed to secure a place when clever Emma had not. No wonder Terri was rattled.

It was an awkward subject to bring up with Mylene and she didn't have a clue how best to do it, but Terri's assertion that Staggs wasn't playing a straight bat was starting to niggle. If Mylene shied away from the topic, perhaps Terri was right, after all.

It was about two o'clock the following afternoon before Bron managed to pop her head round Mylene's door for her 'casual' chat.

'You should have come and had lunch in the canteen,' she said, casting a disapproving eye over the huge green salad Mylene was negotiating with a plastic knife and fork. 'Penne pesto, purple sprouting broccoli and toasted pine nuts.' Bron smacked her lips at the memory. 'A triumph, even if I do say so myself! We've called it 'Crunchy, scrumptious pesto pasta'. There's not a morsel left.'

'Stop it! Your cooking is ruining my figure, Bron, I'll have you know. That's why I'm sitting at my desk, chomping on rabbit food.' Mylene popped a slice of cucumber into her mouth.

Bron had never understood the point of diets. If God had meant women to be thin, he wouldn't have invented magic knickers. Or Gok Wan, for that matter.

'Have you called for something in particular or are you just saying hello? Whichever it is, come right in, I'm not doing anything, as you can see.'

Bron wondered if she must look suspicious, hovering in the doorway awkwardly, neither in nor out, while she tried to think of a way to broach the subject of Jane, and whether she'd got her choice of school or not. Better just to get on with it, she decided. Otherwise the two of them would be here all day.

'I saw Terri yesterday,' she finally blurted out.

Mylene ducked beneath her desk to put her empty lunchbox away in her bag. Rather suspiciously, Bron thought. As if, for some reason, she wanted to hide.

'Oh, yes?' she trilled, from beneath the desk. 'It's been ages since she and I had a proper catch up.'

Her face, when she popped back up into view, was tinged a delicate shade of pink.

'She was saying how thrilled Emma

was that she'd got into Stramley with all her friends.'

Mylene suddenly fixed her eyes on the clock on the wall.

'Good heavens! Is that really the time?' she exclaimed. 'Do you know what, Bron, I've just remembered, I've got a pile of photocopying to do for the Governors' meeting later.'

'Oh, OK then.'

Dumbfounded, Bron turned to go. Being given the brush-off like this hadn't been in her plan. Mylene was supposed to say how pleased she was for Emma, which would be Bron's cue to drop in an innocent enquiry about Jane's destination. All friendly and unthreatening, like. She could hardly ask it now, could she, without looking like she was giving Mylene the third degree?

Anyway, something told her she didn't need to. She was pretty sure she already knew the answer. Terri was right and Bron shouldn't have doubted her. Terri had her ear to the ground and she'd always been nosy. A people person, unlike herself. If there was any gossip going round about Staggs, then Terri would have got to the bottom of it. *Had* got to the bottom of it. Staggs was on the fiddle. If you were useful to him, he'd offer a place to your son or daughter. Otherwise, there were plenty of other schools who would have them.

The adjoining door between Staggs' room and Mylene's office was suddenly flung open to reveal the headmaster himself. Though small in stature; he took pride in making grand entrances. Even before he was properly inside the room, he was barking a set of instructions to Mylene.

How on earth she managed to put up with his inconsiderate manner, Bron couldn't imagine. Words like 'please' and 'thank you' didn't seem to exist in his vocabulary, although it didn't appear to bother Mylene, who couldn't do enough for him. When he'd finally drawn breath enough to concentrate on his surroundings, he spotted her.

'Bron! Didn't see you there. You must be telepathic,' he said. Without waiting for any reaction from Bron to this assertion, he motored on. 'Just made a call. Local paper. Photo opportunity and interview next week some time. For our nomination. Insisted on having *your* number, even though I offered to do the interview myself. Never mind. If it makes you feel more at ease, I can pop down at a moment's notice. Might come better from me. Communication being my forte, and all that.'

A framed picture on the wall provided him with the mirror he needed to check out his appearance. Bron looked on, mesmerised, as he adjusted his jazzy yellow tie in the glass and dusted down the shoulders of his expensive-looking suit.

She loathed having her picture taken. But of one thing she was certain: no way was Staggs going to get his mug in her shot. And if there was an interview to be done, then she was going to be the one to do it. It was time she stood up to Staggs and stopped being so nice about him encroaching on her territory. Especially now, after what she was beginning to suspect about the way he ran his school.

It was with this new sense of determination that Bron went about her business for the rest of the day. She was annoyed with herself that she'd failed in her bid to prise the information she needed from Mylene and she resolved to work on her again the following day. And this time, she'd get straight to the point.

Though what she intended doing about it, even if Mylene admitted that Jane had jumped the queue and managed to grab a place at Poplar Green when others who'd applied hadn't, she still couldn't decide.

Next morning, early, as she made a quick detour from her normal route to visit one of her suppliers before the beginning of the school day, she considered her options. Was Staggs actually breaking the law by cherry-picking prospective students? Bron couldn't be certain, but from where she stood he was certainly breaking a moral code.

A familiar dark green Jag, parked up ahead, drew her attention. Wasn't that Staggs' car? What on earth was he doing parking in the middle of a country lane at this time of the morning?

She'd already driven past and could have continued on her journey, but curiosity made her slow down and pull over to the side of the road some way ahead, where an overhanging bush provided more than adequate cover while at the same time offering the ideal spot from where she could do her snooping unobserved.

She watched as Staggs got out of the car and strolled over to the boot. He disappeared from view for a moment, but when he'd closed the boot, he was revealed to be attempting — rather badly — to put together a fold-up bike.

Bron only knew one person who owned a bike like that. And here she was, climbing out of the passenger seat in a rush to take over Staggs' clumsy efforts. A relieved Staggs relinquished the bike, allowing the woman to complete the task unaided.

Then, glancing at his watch, he gave his companion a quick peck on the cheek, climbed back in the driving seat and drove away, so wrapped up in his own thoughts that he failed to spot Bron's car hidden by trailing leaves at the side of the road.

Bron's eyes returned to Mylene, standing alone in the middle of the country lane, following the car till it disappeared from sight with a wistful, lovelorn gaze. Leaning on her bike, she rested one hand on the cheek that Staggs had just kissed as if she were cherishing the memory of his touch.

So that was the way of it, Bron mused. A love affair. From the perfunctory kiss Staggs had planted on Mylene's cheek, it appeared to mean little, if anything, to him. But clearly, Mylene was a woman in love. And, Bron was certain, a willing accomplice to whatever game Staggs might be playing.

2

The net was closing in around Martin Staggs, though he didn't know it yet. Too many people were talking and rumour was rife. Lucy Lockley, Chief Reporter on *The Bugle*, kept her ear to the ground wherever she went and no scrap of tossed-away gossip was ever wasted on her. But gossip was gossip. You couldn't print it or you'd be taken to court before you could say The Law is an Ass.

That little visit she herself had paid Staggs only last week, in the guise of a fond mama in search of the right kind of educational environment for little Giles, 'my darling son', would never be accepted as proof that Staggs was a wrong 'un, even though she'd played such a blinder that by the end of the interview she'd managed to glean enough on him to ensure he'd never be allowed to run his own school ever again.

A playful smile danced across her lips,

softening her usually stern and intimidating expression. 'Honestly, Lucy, you should have gone on the stage,' she told herself, as, surrounded by the shrill ringing of phones and the raucous banter of her fellow reporters clustering round their computers exchanging news, she relived their conversation.

She'd been right to dress up for her visit to Staggs and never had she been more grateful for those elocution lessons her good old mum had gone out and scrubbed floors to pay for. Staggs was a snob. She'd realised that within seconds of meeting him. If she'd told him she'd been brought up on a council estate and had never been within spitting distance of even a red-brick university, let alone Girton College, Cambridge — which she'd lied about being her alma mater — she doubted he'd have treated her as courteously as he had.

It had taken her no time at all to get the obnoxious creep eating out of her hand. She was a single mother, running her own Internet company and trying to do what was right by her son, she explained. Probably she'd left it too late to find the perfect school for Giles for September and she felt really bad about that, but working twenty-four-seven as she did, in order to keep the millions rolling in, had always meant poor Giles had got used to having to come second.

At the mention of millions, Staggs' eyes had practically popped out on stalks. Of course there'd be a place for Giles, he'd panted, without a single enquiry about the boy's educational level even being raised. Phew! That was a relief, she'd gasped. She'd been so worried that her son might be asked to sit some sort of entrance exam. Which would have been a disaster, since the poor boy had trouble sitting still for long enough to write his name at the top of the paper, and as for spelling and sums well, the least said about those two things the better!

To give him credit, Staggs did have the grace to register some discomfort at this point. But he was a man skilled in the art of thinking on his feet, Lucy could see. By law, he said, every child was indeed required to take an entrance test if they wanted a place at Poplar Green. But in some circumstances . . . Quick as a flash, Lucy spotted the bait on the end of his hook and was on to it.

She could be very generous, she hinted, when it came to financial matters, should it fall to Mr Staggs to be kind enough to let dear little Giles into his charming school. If it was cash he needed for an extension to the playing field, for example, or perhaps a new wing for the library, well, he need look no further. Staggs didn't exactly rub his hands in glee at this point but she had no doubt he'd be doing it once she'd gone. In no time, she'd made a further appointment for herself and Giles to come back and have another look round, so he could see the school for himself.

He'll absolutely love it here, Staggs gushed as he took her hand in his to seal the deal, before personally showing her out.

Oh, absolutely, she gushed back. *She was sure he would*. If he'd ever existed, that is — which, of course, he hadn't.

Back in the present, Lucy checked the

telephone number young Jim Thomas had passed on to her. What a stroke of luck they'd bumped into each other as she'd been going out and he'd been coming in, after his visit to Poplar Green to interview the school cook, who'd been nominated for some award or other.

That man is an egomaniac, he'd said, when she'd brought up Staggs' name and asked Jim if he'd happened to meet him. *He wants that trophy for himself, believe me. The way he pushed that poor woman aside every time I asked her a question had to be seen to be believed. Not to mention showing off at every opportunity about where his school is in the league tables and how many of the sixth form will be going to Oxbridge. I felt like telling him if he wanted publicity, then he was going to have to pay for an advert, but that, actually, I'd come to speak to the school cook not him!*

Yes, without a doubt, the Fates had delivered Bronwen Wright to her door. What she needed was *hard* evidence not gossip, and Bronwen, as an insider, was the woman who could get that evidence for her. Once Lucy filled her in on her suspicions, she was confident Bronwen, clearly no fan of Staggs, from the barely contained rage in her face in the photo on the cover of the latest issue of *The Bugle*, would be chafing at the bit. Lucy lifted the receiver and began to dial.

★   ★   ★

Bron gazed at her own grainy black-and-white image slap bang in the middle of the front page of *The Bugle* and sank her head in her hands despairingly. Her chef's hat was awry, and wasn't that a gravy stain on her apron? Both those things were bad enough, but it was the expression on her face that made her wish she could intercept every single copy of *The Bugle* before it landed on everyone's doormat, so that she could shred the whole damn lot.

It was Staggs' fault. Until he turned up to steal the limelight, she'd been getting on like a house on fire with the lad they'd sent to snap her. Cheeky blighter, he was, eyeing her newly-baked scones and hinting how well one would go down with the nice cup of tea she might be thinking about offering him, before they got stuck into the photo session.

Yet somewhere, mixed in with his cheek, was a huge dollop of charm. It convinced her that having a camera pointed at her might not be as bad as she feared. In fact, his compliments on her baking combined with his silly joke about Nigella Lawson having to watch her back, convinced her it might even be fun. And then Staggs had come bursting into the kitchen, in that egomaniacal way of his.

From that moment, it had all gone pear-shaped. Sensing a change in the pecking order, that young whipper-snapper of a photographer had quickly switched allegiance from Bron to Staggs in less time than it took him to point his camera at them and say *Smile, please*, falling for Staggs' patter like a gambler at the races who'd just been given a winning tip.

The results of Staggs' coup were now all too evident in the photograph before her. There he was, all smiles and geniality, dressed in a suit and tie she certainly hadn't seen before and wouldn't have been surprised to discover he'd bought expressly for the purpose. And there she was. Glaring straight ahead, her mouth looking like it had been stretched by a coat hanger into a terrifying grimace, she looked like one of the undead. All that was missing were the wires coming out of her neck.

Folding the newspaper up, she dropped it in the bin with a sigh and reminded herself that by the weekend people would be eating their fish and chips out of it and, even better, by the time the next issue of *The Bugle* came out this picture would be a distant memory.

The phone rang and she jumped a mile. What if Terri had got hold of a copy and was ringing to berate her for bringing shame on the good name of the entire House of Wright in a single camera flash? But the person on the other end of the line turned out to be a stranger to her. She introduced herself as Lucy Lockley from *The Bugle*. Bron had a sudden memory of her byline, beneath a small picture of a stern yet glamorous woman with a fringe.

'I've just seen your photograph and read your story,' she said, sounding, to Bron's ears, very posh and rather scary as a result.

'Oh,' Bron replied.

Under the circumstances, there was little else she could say, she decided. She could hardly deny that the woman in the picture was herself, much as she would have liked to.

'You don't look very happy in it.'

'I was,' Bron said. 'Only I'd forgotten to tell my face so.'

A warm chuckle from down the line relaxed Bron a little.

'It's a nice story,' Lucy Lockley said. 'So nice, in fact, that I wondered if I could do a piece about you.'

'What, *another* piece?' Bron was puzzled. 'There's already three paragraphs about me! I'd have thought that was more than enough for anyone.'

There was a long pause before Lucy Lockley spoke again.

'OK, Bron. I'll come clean. I shouldn't

have tried to trick you in the first place.' She lowered her voice so that Bron had to strain to hear what she said next. 'The truth is I'd like to talk to you about your headmaster.'

'What, Staggs?'

Suddenly, Bron felt angry and used. She'd tried to keep her petty feelings of jealousy at bay, but it was no use. Staggs had set out to snatch the glory of her nomination from under her nose almost from the moment it had become public knowledge. He'd done an excellent job on that photographer, weaselling his way into her photo shoot, and now he'd managed to get none other than Lucy Lockley, *The Bugle's* ace reporter, hanging on his words, too.

'I suggest that if you want to speak to Mr Staggs, you ring his PA,' she said coldly.

Another pause, then, 'You don't like him, do you, Bron?'

'He's my boss,' Bron said.

It was no answer, but she had no intentions of perjuring herself to a reporter, of all people.

'Bron.' Ms Lockley's tone suddenly became confidential. 'I've been in this business a long time and I'm not usually wrong about people. And I am certain that my instinct about you is spot on. As soon as I saw that photo, I felt the hairs on the back of my neck prickle.'

'Well, I'll be the first to admit I'm no oil painting, but all the same!' Bron was so irate that her words came out in a squeak.

Immediately, Lucy Lockley jumped in with an apology. By no means had she meant to insult Bron, she insisted. Far from it. She'd like to offer her sincerest congratulations on a well-deserved nomination. Bron thawed a little at the compliment. In fact, in celebration and to make up for her tactlessness, what if Bron let her treat her to tea at Dorrington's? At the mention of Dorrington's, Bron cheered up even more. Everything there was delicious and their apple Danish, in particular, were out of this world.

It might be nice to get out of town following work after all, she decided. It would certainly be a way of avoiding

Terri for a couple of hours, or anyone else who might have seen her on *The Bugle's* front page, for that matter. Besides, she was curious to know the real reason Lucy Lockley had invited her for tea.

* ★ ★ ★ *

Lucy liked to arrive at a rendezvous first, if at all possible. That way she could bag the quietest table and give herself time to scan the menu so that she could make a suggestion about the best thing to order, without the other person wasting precious time trying to choose between several different options and being unable to come to a decision. Never having been one herself, Lucy had little patience with ditherers.

She looked up from the menu as a small, apple-shaped woman in an ill-fitting beige jacket and sensible shoes came bustling through the tea-room door. Unless she was mistaken, this was Bronwen. An apple Danish woman, she decided, beaming at the approaching figure, or she wasn't worth that humungous rise in her salary she'd just negotiated.

Half an hour, one apple Danish and two cappuccinos later, Bron had pledged allegiance to Lucy's cause. She truly hadn't meant to spill out the story of her visit to Terri yesterday but there was something so charismatic about Lucy that it was impossible to keep it back. In no time at all she found herself revealing how, at first, she'd refused to take seriously Terri's accusation that Staggs was cherry-picking his pupils depending on where they lived and who their parents were. Since she'd had more time to think it over, though, she wondered if maybe there was at least a grain of truth in her daughter's suspicions.

Even the teacher had been surprised that Emma, who everybody knew was as bright as a button, had failed the entrance exam, she told a fascinated Lucy. Whereas Ben Fielding, who was no brighter, but who happened to have a local councillor as a father, had romped through it.

Lucy's ears had pricked up at the mention of that particular snippet of information. Of course, Bron hadn't *completely* let down her guard. She wasn't an idiot. She had no intention of sharing Terri's suggestion that Bron should use her influence — such as it was — with Staggs and get him to change his mind about refusing her granddaughter a place at Poplar Green. The mere memory of Terri's outburst still made her shudder with distaste that it should even cross Terri's mind.

'I'm still not sure what it is you want me to do exactly,' Bron said, wishing she hadn't guzzled her Danish so quickly, because now she had to sit there and watch Lucy Lockley pick her way through the one on her plate like a little bird.

'Keep your eyes and ears open, that's all. Do a bit of snooping. Do you ever get a chance to be alone in his room?'

Bron stared open-mouthed at Lucy. Had she any idea what she was asking?

'If I wanted to do that I'd have to go through Mylene. And I'd have to shoot her first,' she joked.

'Ah, yes. The PA. Pretty name. Pretty woman, too. Almost stylish.'

Bron coloured up as she remembered the forlorn expression on Mylene's face yesterday morning, standing in the middle of the deserted country road and staring longingly after Staggs' car, until it was out of sight.

'Do you think there's anything going on there?'

Lucy's question came out of the blue, leading Bron to quickly work out why it was the other woman and not herself who was the journalist.

'No matter,' she said. 'I can see you're uncomfortable with the question and besides, I don't suppose it's relevant. Though she could do far better than him, if you ask me.' Fixing Bron with her gimlet eye, she added, 'So, Bron. Will you help me?'

Bron thought about it. She was going to have to be careful. And she was going to have to be clever. But why not give it a go? If Staggs was up to something, then Lucy was right. It was in the public interest to expose it.

Days passed and Bron felt she was getting nowhere. She'd been stupid to fall for Lucy Lockley's fine talk of *all for the public good*, she decided one morning as she strode around the kitchen deep in thought.

She was meant to be inventing a new and exciting pudding to celebrate Year Nine's spectacular success in the inter-county debating competition. She rather liked the idea of lots of different flavours, all jostling to be tasted. Already she had a name for it — *Argumentative Trifle*, suggested by one of the children on the tasting team. All she had to do now was to work out what to put in it before Friday, when the trophy was to be presented.

Just as the word *trophy* popped into her head, Bron dropped the pile of recipe books she was in the middle of transferring from one corner of the room to another, with a loud clatter.

'You all right, Bron?' Annette looked up from the sauce she was stirring. 'You look like you've seen a ghost!'

'Been struck by inspiration more like,' Sandra suggested from the sink.

'I'd say you were spot on, Sandra,' Bron said, dropping to her knees to retrieve the books. 'I do believe I'm finally getting somewhere.'

And with that, she scooped up the books, set them untidily down on a spare bit of space and excused herself. There was an old friend of hers she hadn't spoken to for ages who she was suddenly desperate to get back in contact with . . .

★ ★ ★

Bron couldn't believe her good fortune. Not only was Staggs out for the afternoon, but Mylene had dashed off to pick up her daughter from school, after a call informing her she was complaining of a sore throat.

'It's really good of you to let me into his room while he's out,' Bron said, trotting behind school caretaker Len in the direction of Staggs' office. 'Silly me, leaving my next week's recipes with him.

And it's no use me trying to ring the suppliers and do my ordering from memory.'

Len smiled at her indulgently as he let her in. From the way he was hovering, he looked like he might be thinking of coming in with her, which wouldn't do at all.

'Off you go, Len,' she said firmly. 'I've wasted enough of your time already and I'm sure you've got lots to get on with. I'll take the keys and lock up after myself, if you like. Drop them off later.'

Len looked horrified at the prospect of being parted from his precious keys. If it was all the same to her, he'd come back later, he said. She could give him a ring when she'd found what she wanted. It was a relief to shut the door after him. Len was a lovely man but Staggs could turn up at any moment and she was a woman on a mission.

Though what that mission was she couldn't say. What exactly was incriminating evidence? On every shelf stacks of important-looking files jostled for space. No way could Lucy Lockley expect her to rummage through all of those. And then there were the cupboards.

Each one locked, so totally out of bounds, thank goodness, because, frankly, the thought of having to check every single piece of paper no doubt contained therein defeated her.

Cautiously, her heart thumping, straining her ears for the telltale ring of Staggs' footsteps, she approached his desk. Everything seemed as it should be. Phone, computer, trays marked *IN* and *OUT*, a plastic holder full of pens, a buff folder marked *ENTRANCE EXAMINATION — RESULTS*.

Well, if she was going to start anywhere here was good enough, she decided. Maybe she could check up on Emma's marks — put Terri's mind at rest. Her shaking fingers inched towards the folder. As she lifted it, a piece of paper fell out and drifted down on to the ground. Bron bent down to retrieve it.

It was a note, written in a scrawl that Bron recognised as belonging to Staggs, addressed to Mylene. Groping for the glasses that she kept on a chain round her neck, Bron fumbled to put them on before struggling to decipher Staggs' words. Initially, it was hard to grasp what, exactly, was meant by all those abbreviations and cryptic numbers. But once she'd read it back, the full significance began to sink in.

Mylene, she read. *Just a couple of alterations. Page 4. St Cuthbert's Primary. Bradley Smith for Carrie Scoones. Mother a GP, father top oncology man at The General. (Besides there's only 6 in it.) Ditto, page 5 — Staines Road Primary. Emma Cameron for Ben Fielding. (2.) Please remember to change the pencil marks on the page before you enter them on the computer, to be on the safe side.*

When she saw Emma's name, side by side with Ben Fielding's, she caught her breath. What did that figure 2 in brackets mean? she wondered. Well, there was only one way to find out. All fingers and thumbs, she groped her way to page five. There was a list of names — all the children in the two classes of year six, who'd taken the entrance exam for a place at Poplar Green. Fifteen in all. There was Mylene's daughter's name — Jane — with a score of 48% crossed out and changed to a much more convincing 84. And there was Emma's name just above the name of Ben Fielding, the politician's son, with a pencil arrow suggesting the scores be reversed.

Suddenly the door burst open. Bron spun round. It was Staggs, his hand on the doorknob, fixing her with a menacing look.

'What, may I ask, are you doing, sneaking around in my office?'

He'd seen the folder in her hand. Rigid with terror, all Bron could do was watch his face as the full realisation of what she must have discovered sank in. He stood stock still for a moment, considering what to do next, the only movement the throbbing of a muscle in his cheek.

'I can explain,' she croaked, as, stirred into action at last, he began to stride towards her.

3

Sandra and Annette were taking advantage of the post-lunchtime lull by sharing a pot of tea when Bron, out of breath, her chef's hat slipping down over one eye, came sprinting into the kitchen.

'Tea, quick,' Bron gasped. 'Plenty of milk.'

Quick as a flash, Annette jumped up, grabbed a spare mug and filled it to the brim while Sandra tore open a new packet of bourbons. If they imagined such a speedy and generous response entitled them to an explanation for her dishevelled appearance, Bron was going to have to disappoint them. How could she possibly explain that she'd been poking about in Staggs' office looking for evidence that he was up to no good? Or that, just as she thought she'd found it, he'd caught her red-handed?

She never thought she'd be so relieved to hear the familiar sound of Len's keys as he came jangling along the corridor. She could have hugged him when, with his brisk knock, coupled with his call of, 'Are you decent?' Len's face appeared round the door. Immediately Staggs, flustered by the interruption, backed right away from her. What would have happened had Len not chosen that exact moment to breeze into the room, Bron refused even to contemplate. For now she was safe, but she didn't fancy being alone with Staggs again any time soon — that was for sure.

After slaking her thirst and fixing her sugar craving with two biscuits in rapid succession, she decided to ring Lucy Lockley right away. She needed to check her inbox, too, in case Pieter had already got round to replying to the e-mail she'd asked her old college friend, Mary, to forward to him in South Africa. She just prayed that Mary was still in touch with Pieter, or this particular avenue of investigation would be closed to her.

'I'll be in my office,' she said, through a mouthful of crumbs. 'And if Staggs comes prowling round, I am absolutely not here.'

* * *

Good! Pieter had indeed received it and already replied. His tone was friendly if a little guarded, Bron thought, skimming through it. He lost no opportunity to mention his wife, she noticed. Did he really think she'd made contact in order to let him know she was still available if he fancied giving it another go? Honestly, the ego of the man.

'Get over yourself, Pieter,' she muttered. 'I did — more than thirty years ago.'

Swiftly, she read on.

Fancy you remembering that when I came back home to South Africa after catering college, it was to a teaching position at Krakenthorp High School I returned.

'Not surprising at all,' Bron muttered. They'd had huge rows about it. It was what broke them up in the end. Pieter was a genius in the kitchen. As top of the

48

class of '74, he'd been offered lots of opportunities to work with Michelin-starred chefs throughout Europe. But he'd turned them all down in favour of a boring teaching job in the same school he'd attended as a boy.

His country needed him, he insisted, and teaching wouldn't make the same demands on him that working in a restaurant would. He needed his evenings to take part in the struggle against apartheid, was how he put it. Bron called him all the names under the sun for throwing away opportunities other students would kill for. She was young and politics meant even less to her in those days than they did now. She accused him of bottling it, of not being up to the challenge.

But she'd been wrong, she realised, as soon as she'd finished reading the rest of his e-mail. Pieter could have turned his back on South Africa but he'd chosen not to. He'd done his bit to change the country and now he was running a successful chain of restaurants, where a person's skin colour was of no consequence.

Bron gave herself a mental nudge. She had things to do. A phone call to make to *The Bugle* in the hope that Lucy was at her desk and another e-mail to write to Pieter, now she was certain that the name of the school he'd once taught at was indeed the same name she'd seen on the trophy on the filing cabinet in Staggs' room.

Funny how that trophy had been in his room as long as he'd been headmaster, but the significance of the name Krakenthorp engraved on it had only occurred to her last week, while she was in the school kitchen. She'd been in the middle of creating a new recipe for a special pudding she'd been asked to make in honour of the school's brilliant victory in the intercounty debating championship. Out of the blue, her mind had hopped from pudding to trophy, from trophy to Krakenthorp and thence to Pieter, whom she hadn't thought of for years. What if Pieter had run across Staggs during his time there? She didn't know if he had, but she knew how to find out. In no time at all she'd contacted Mary, secretary of her old catering college's ex-alumni association, and got her to pass on her message.

Now that she'd re-established contact with Pieter, she was in the perfect position to find out if he'd known Staggs, and if he had, then sound him out about his past. Had he always been ambitious and self-serving, for instance? Or had he been a regular guy once upon a time and the change in him only occurred after a few months in his new appointment as principal of Poplar Green?

Maybe he just woke up one morning and decided that if he couldn't make his school the best in the county by fair means then he'd do it by foul ones. And if that meant that only the children of the rich and well-connected got places, then so be it. Never mind the kids from the council estate, because unless their parents could finance half-a-dozen brand-new, state-of-the-art computers, or offer a couple of grand towards a new language lab, then the riff-raff could just go elsewhere!

Even if the two men's paths had never

crossed, Bron was determined to leave no stone unturned. Scanning *The Bugle's* photo into her computer, she hoped fervently that this picture of the two of them might jog Pieter's memory. Anything that might reveal Staggs to have had the makings of a crook could only add weight to the body of evidence Bron needed to expose him.

* * *

Thanks to a phone call from Jane's school, Mylene had missed her lunch break and now, back at her desk, her stomach growled with hunger. There hadn't even been anything wrong with Jane, when she'd finally arrived at school, that she could see. But the headmistress had fixed her with such an accusing look when she'd said as much that Mylene felt obliged to take Jane straight home, where she'd fixed her up with a dose of Calpol and made up her bed on the settee in front of a DVD, warning her to open the door to no one until she herself returned in two hours' time.

Driving back to school, a niggling headache already setting in which Mylene put down to the fact that her blood sugar was low — it had been her intention to quickly get through any urgent business before leaving early with work she could do at home. Of course, that plan was always going to depend on Martin's generosity. And you didn't need to be a genius to realise that right now, as he came charging into her room with a face like thunder, was probably not the best time to ask him for a favour.

The sight of Martin's aggressive manner, his cheeks purple with rage, as he came bearing down on her, waving a buff-coloured folder in front of her nose while accusing her of stupidity and incompetence, filled her with near terror. What had happened to provoke him like this?

'What were you thinking of, leaving *this* on my desk for all the world to see?' he yelled, before rapidly explaining how, less than an hour ago, he'd arrived back from his meeting, walked into his office and caught Bron flicking through the folder that contained the exam entrance-test results.

Mylene caught the folder as he flung it on her desk. A single sheet of paper escaped, landing on the floor, and she reached down to retrieve it. Her heart sank as she recognised its contents — Martin's amendments to the list of names she herself had typed. Emma Cameron's name crossed out and replaced by that of Ben Fielding, a boy who'd scored two marks less than Emma. And worse, if there could possibly be worse — her own daughter's marks reversed, so that instead of appearing average, they looked brilliant.

She'd seen this sheet of paper before, of course. It had been her job to transcribe the information on to a new computer file and to make sure that the paper evidence was completely shredded. How could she have been so stupid as to leave it there for anyone to read?

Immediately, her mind turned to Bron. If she'd had the file in her hand long enough to read Emma's name and register the fact that Jane's right to a scholarship had been snatched from under her nose, then she wasn't going to leave it at that, was she?

What if she'd already called the police and reported her suspicions? Of course, it might be that Martin's sudden interruption had taken her by surprise before she'd managed to make sense of his hieroglyphics. But how would they know either way? The only thing they could do was sit and wait it out. But for how long?

Images of her daughter flashed before her eyes. It was for Jane she'd done this, not for herself. If Martin hadn't suggested how convenient she'd find it having her daughter at the same school where she worked, so she could keep an eye on her, there was no way she'd ever have entertained the idea of helping him in his fraudulent behaviour.

'I only did what you asked me to do,' she croaked, gazing up at Staggs with tear-filled eyes.

Staggs threw back his head and let out a mirthless laugh.

'Please don't tell me you are thinking of using the excuse that you were only obeying orders, Mylene.' Staggs' tone grew suddenly weary. 'Because you are just as guilty in this as I am and any court would see it.'

Mylene had noticed the sudden change in Martin's voice. Gone was the playfulness he sometimes employed when they were alone and in its place was a gruffness she'd only ever heard before on those occasions when he'd addressed a member of staff, or a child who'd displeased him. She decided his change in manner towards her was just a temporary blip, brought on by sudden panic, and she wouldn't let it affect the way she spoke to him.

'What are we going to do?'

Martin was all-powerful in this school — it had been that which had first attracted her to him. Surely he could think of a way out of this terrible mess.

'With Bron, you mean?'

Mylene gave a tinkly little laugh to mask her discomfort. *With* Bron suggested something vaguely sinister. As soon as the thought occurred to her, she tried to dismiss it. A slip of the tongue on

Martin's part, that's all. She'd meant *about* Bron, obviously, she said.

Couldn't he just get her in the office, talk her round? After all, she didn't have the evidence, did she? *They* had it.

She jumped up from her desk, strode over to the shredder in the corner of the room and quickly fed it through the teeth of the machine.

'There,' she said. 'All done. She's got nothing on us any more.'

But Martin didn't seem to be listening. It was as if he was miles away, staring into space, arms crossed over his chest, tapping his fingers to a steady rhythm on the sleeve of his jacket.

★   ★   ★

Bron didn't feel safe in her office, now Annette and Sandra had gone home. It was four o'clock. Soon everyone would be off-site. She could go home, too, but she didn't have a computer there and she was anxious to discover what Pieter had to tell her — if anything — about Staggs.

For the umpteenth time, since she'd

first caught sight of it, she turned her mind to that innocuous-looking folder marked *ENTRANCE EXAMINATION — RESULTS,* desperately trying to dredge up the details on the page. She was getting old, she decided. Her memory wasn't as good as it once was. And with Staggs barging in like that, putting the fear of God into her — no wonder it had driven everything she'd just read right out of her mind.

Not quite everything, though. Emma's name had been there, plain as a pikestaff. And so had Ben Fielding's. And there had been something fishy about Emma's marks, too, unless she was very much mistaken.

The exact wording had escaped her, she'd told Lucy Lockley earlier in a phone call, but it looked very much like Staggs had been swapping all the marks around. When she added that it looked as if the secretary's daughter, who'd scored badly, had been given the scholarship that rightly should have gone to her own granddaughter, Lucy's reaction seemed gleeful.

'You've done brilliantly, Bron. And now we've got this evidence to take to the police, there's no way Staggs will be able to wriggle out of it.'

It had all gone a bit pear-shaped after Bron said that, actually, she'd left the evidence in Staggs' room and fled.

'I was terrified,' she said, in an attempt to justify her actions to the rather cold silence that had suddenly developed on the end of the line. 'I was convinced he was about to go for me. If the caretaker hadn't appeared just then . . . '

The sniff of disdain coming from Ms Lockley was a really bad sign, Bron decided. There'd be no more cappuccinos and apple Danishes at Dorringtons' for her. With a brusque thank-you for her time, *The Bugle's* ace reporter rang off, leaving Bron feeling more than slightly humiliated.

But she had no intentions of giving up. She'd never been a quitter and if there was more evidence to be had about Staggs, then she'd find it. She owed it to her granddaughter and to all the other children Staggs had done the dirty on, just because he didn't like the sound of their postcode.

She didn't fancy staying here on her own, though; the last of the stragglers were drifting home. Soon the staff room would be empty. She suddenly remembered that Len had a computer with Internet access. She'd feel safe with Len in his little den.

★   ★   ★

Len listened to her story without interruption, while busying himself making coffee, allowing her to take her time and agreeing that unless she told it her own way, she'd get muddled. He hadn't once tried to rush her — not even when she took a bit of a detour describing what she thought was the secret ingredient that put Dorringtons' apple Danishes in a class of their own.

'Well, we can't leave it there,' Len said, while handing Bron her coffee. 'Just because you left the evidence behind doesn't mean we let Staggs get away with it.'

'He'll have shredded it by now,' Bron said dolefully. 'Or rather, he'll have got Mylene to do it. Who'd have thought a nice girl like that would be in cahoots with a rogue like Staggs?'

'There's no accounting for taste in affairs of the heart,' Len said.

Bron shifted uneasily in her chair. When she'd explained about Pieter, and what they'd once meant to each other, he remarked how he'd always thought that the memory of first love remained with us even in old age.

His own first love had died in a road accident, he'd said, and he still thought of her from time to time. Bron's heart went out to him. She felt honoured that he'd wanted to share this information with her. For the first time, she felt Len was more friend than colleague and sensed he felt the same. But even so, the silence that followed was getting a bit intense.

'I'll check again to see if Pieter's got back to me,' Bron said, setting down her mug and typing her password into the computer.

'Bingo!' Len said, peering over her

shoulder as Pieter's name showed up in her inbox.

They read in silence, Bron glancing up occasionally to check Len was keeping pace before scrolling down the page. Now the atmosphere in the office was electric, both of them holding their breath as the full significance of Pieter's words hit home. What he told them was far worse than any suspicion of fraud they might have on Staggs, they realised.

When they heard faint footsteps coming down the corridor outside, they stiffened. Instinctively, Bron shut down the computer. Len saw the fear in her eyes as Staggs' voice boomed out.

'Len. I'm looking for Bron. I thought she might be down here.'

Len put his fingers to his lips. The slightest noise could give them both away.

'It'll be OK,' he mouthed, gently rubbing her shoulder.

She looked up at him with such trust that it filled him with confidence. It *would* be OK. This was *his* patch.

Outside, Staggs' footsteps faltered. The basement was a warren and Staggs wouldn't have the first idea where to start looking for him. Len, on the other hand, knew this part of the school like the back of his hand. Grasping the bunch of keys with both hands to muffle any jangling, he moved towards the door on silent feet.

Staggs was some way down the corridor, tugging at each door as he walked hurriedly past. He was carrying something in his hand — it looked like a tea towel. What was he thinking of doing with that? Len wondered, before the full horror of the uses one could put a tea towel to sank in.

Now Staggs had his hand on the handle of the cleaner's closet. Len selected a key. What a piece of luck! The biggest, fanciest key for the smallest, skankiest room in the whole school.

Staggs was trying that door now. He peered cautiously round it, calling Len's name again. Demanding to know if he'd seen Bron because he needed to find her urgently. Len crept up behind him, startling his quarry. The push he gave Staggs sent the smaller, lighter man reeling headlong into the cramped space.

Len quickly slammed the door behind him and turned the key. The sound of a distraught Staggs hammering on the door to be let out brought Bron running to the scene, where she witnessed a rather smug-looking Len, leaning with his back against the door and grinning gleefully.

'Oh, thank God!' she cried. 'I thought it might be the other way round.'

★ ★ ★

The new headmaster, Mr Stocks, wouldn't hear a word of Bron's objection that maybe it wouldn't be in very good taste to spend the evening partying at a posh hotel in London, after the news had leaked to the nationals that Martin Staggs, headmaster of Poplar Green Independent School, was not and never had been Martin Staggs in the first place, but Lance Koenig, a classroom assistant at a small school in Johannesburg, South Africa.

Bron had won *Best School Grub Award* fairly and squarely and she would be letting a lot of people down if she refused to accept it on — as far as he was concerned, anyway — some questionable principle. It might have been her friend in South Africa who'd recognised the man in the photo she'd sent him as Koenig, but if Bron hadn't had her suspicions in the first place, the truth may never have come out.

So here they were, the six of them — all slightly drunk on champagne and success. Bron was glad she had invited Len instead of Terri — who'd been dropping hints for weeks — especially as Annette and Sandra had decided to bring their partners, after all. Len looked quite dapper in his DJ, she thought, as she raised her glass to him.

What they'd discovered back in Len's office that afternoon had brought them closer. Pieter's e-mail had revealed that the real Staggs had been a popular teacher, and a natural leader. But, one day, he simply disappeared without trace. Coincidentally, some twenty-four hours later, Koenig, a man disliked by both students and staff, also disappeared. Pieter vaguely remembered the police being involved, but nothing came of it. In time, the rumour spread that the two men had probably wandered off into the bush and been mauled to death by lions.

Bron's e-mail, and the photo of the man he knew without doubt was Koenig and not Staggs, had triggered Pieter's memory. Once the South African police were alerted, the case was reopened and Koenig was arrested and charged with having murdered the real Staggs in a fit of jealousy-fuelled rage.

'To Mylene and Koenig,' Len said. 'I sincerely hope they're enjoying their porridge.'

'And to Emma, wishing her good luck in her first term at Poplar Green,' Bron added.

'Rightfully deserved,' Len said. 'Just like your award.'

It had gone quiet at their table and Bron felt everyone's eyes on her and Len. It suddenly occurred to her that Sandra and Annette would never let her forget this come Monday morning.

She grinned at them, feeling suddenly reckless. Never mind about Monday, she thought. It would come soon enough.

Right now it was Saturday night and she was having the time of her life.

'How's about another one of these?' she said, waving the empty bottle in the air.

Making a Difference

1

Shelley Lansdown approached the row of houseboats with trepidation. A few people were already up and about — swabbing the deck, Shelley guessed, or whatever it was people who lived on boats did first thing in a morning. They raised their heads at the sight of the small, fair-haired woman in the blue uniform and hat — the initials PCSO picked out in white lettering on her navy jacket — and either nodded a greeting or threw her a suspicious glance.

However they reacted, Shelley returned their look with a warm smile. *A Police Community Support Officer is the friendly, reassuring face of policing,* she remembered from her training. Some people were suspicious of anyone in uniform — her own mother, who she was about to drop in on, among them. But Shelley, a born optimist, was convinced you could win anyone round with a smile.

Ahead lay *Milarepa,* her mother Ruby's boat, sparkling in the morning sunlight — a psychedelic swirl of bright colours that elevated it far above the drab green and brown of the boats moored on either side of it.

Unlike some of her floating neighbours, Ruby was nowhere to be seen. Cautiously, Shelley stepped on deck and tapped at her mother's door. Better get this over with once and for all, she'd decided that morning as, tweaking the hat she was convinced made her head look like a squashed cabbage, she'd stood in front of the mirror and checked her appearance for one last time before leaving the house.

'Ruby! It's me. Shelley. Are you up?' she called.

From inside, she heard movement, followed by the chink of the padlock and the groan of the bolt as it was pulled back. Then Ruby flung open the door, her mass of white hair tumbling over her shoulders.

'My God!' Her hand flew to her mouth at the sight of Shelley in uniform.

Shelley had expected this reaction. Sometimes it was hard to decide who was the most dramatic female in her family, her mother or her daughter. Right now, she'd plump for Ruby, since the only reaction she'd had from seventeen-year-old Heather had been a strangled snigger as she'd been leaving for college, where she was enrolled on a hairdressing course.

''Allo, 'allo, 'allo,' Shelley said, arms behind her back and flexing her knees, in a bid to inject some humour into the situation.

Her mother stuck her head round the door and peered outside. 'Are you coming in?' she hissed. 'I wouldn't want the neighbours seeing you. They'd think I was snooping on them.'

'Nice friends you've got, Mum,' Shelley said. 'Unless they're doing something illegal, they've got nothing to worry about.'

Ruby, who loathed the word 'mum' and any variation of it, shuddered.

'It's to do with their civil liberties. Not that we've got any of those any more.' She sighed wearily. 'Or that you'd give two hoots about them anyway, Starling, now you're part of the police force.'

This time, it was Shelley's turn to shudder. Starling was the name on her birth certificate, but she'd dropped it long before she'd got to secondary school, having already suffered enough at primary school. No one likes to be called Tweety Pie, after all. Her own children had sensible names — Heather and Nathan — and, if ever they complained about them, she lost no opportunity to remind them of some of the alternatives their granny had suggested. That soon shut them up.

'Listen, Ruby,' she said. 'I'm not here to pick a fight. I'm on my way to work. My first day unsupervised. Waterside's halfway between home and Burroway — that's my beat — so I thought I'd just drop by to say hello, because I haven't seen you in a while.'

This seemed to calm her mother. The fire in her eyes that lit up Ruby's face whenever she got a bee in her bonnet about something — be it women's rights or the environment or politics back in her

Greenham Common days — dimmed slightly.

'Yes, well, I suppose I haven't seen much of you since you started your training. All that marching about and clubbing innocent people over the head with batons must be exhausting. I can quite understand why you wouldn't want to come out again in the evening, once you'd got home and put your feet up.'

'Oh, Ruby,' Shelley protested. 'We don't march and we don't practise beating people up, as well you know. We're there for the public — to make them feel safer — and to support the police, so they can get on with their job.'

Ruby nodded, unconvinced. 'All very admirable, I'm sure, darling,' she said. 'And what about the children? Are they in favour of your new job?'

That was a tricky one. Nathan was fine about it. She'd be earning good money for the first time in her life and there would be lots in it for him — a computer at last, for one thing.

At thirteen, he was so far indifferent to image. He'd simply said she looked fine in her uniform and that she should take no notice of Heather's remark that the stab vest she had to wear made her look like a teddy bear — adding that *he* thought a stab vest was really cool, actually, bless him.

'They're fine with it,' Shelley said curtly, adding that the important thing was that it was something she wanted to do for herself, after years of bringing up two children single-handed, on no money apart from a widow's pension.

'Glyn's been dead three years now,' she added. 'It's time I moved on. It won't be long before Nathan and Heather are off my hands. I need to start investing in myself now, while I'm still young enough to embark on a career.'

'I'm sure you're right, Starling,' Ruby said. 'But there are other things in life besides a career, remember. You never know, you might meet a nice man now you've got yourself a job.'

'The only men I'm likely to meet are criminals!' Shelley said with a chuckle.

Turning to leave, she spotted an overturned earthenware pot, from which a handful of peat had spilled. A crimson geranium, its petals scattered and its stem broken, lay beside it.

'Oh, dear,' Shelley said. 'What happened there?'

Ruby followed Shelley's gaze and her face fell when she saw the damaged pot plant.

'Do you want me to sweep it up before I go?'

Ruby shook her head, her lips tight. She seemed shaken, Shelley thought, and angry, too.

'No, you go. Don't want to be late on your first big day. It's my fault. I ought to have brought it inside last night. No doubt some drunken yob thought it was a good idea to destroy it on his way back from the pub.'

'Do you get a lot of drunken yobs round here at night?'

She worried about her mother living here on Waterside, no matter how often Ruby reassured her about the strong community spirit among the boat-dwellers.

'Oh, you know. Now and then. There's

antisocial behaviour everywhere these days, isn't there?' Then, in a complete change of mood, and presenting her cheek for a kiss, she told Shelley it had been lovely to see her but she really had to get on. Ruby had always been expert at getting rid of unwanted guests, Shelley mused, as she hopped back on to dry land.

Shelley's office was a box of a room tucked deep inside the bowels of Burroway Community Centre, with only a computer, a desk and a couple of chairs as furniture. A picture might be nice, and a few photos — to make it more homely, she thought — and logged in to see what crimes, if any, had occurred on her beat overnight and where her presence might be most useful.

Apart from one report of antisocial behaviour — kids at a loose end gathering outside the local shop and making a nuisance of themselves, and a request for her presence at the local allotment to talk to a Mr Peter Farlow, the Chairman of the Allotment Society, about an incident of theft, there was nothing that jumped out at Shelley today. There was also an e-mail from the newly appointed Community Beat Officer, a PC Quinn — who she hadn't yet met — wishing her good luck on her first day unsupervised and saying that he'd be along later to introduce himself, unless something urgent cropped up.

She decided a visit to George and Elsie Butterworth would be the most useful thing she could do. Last week, they'd had a break-in, and though very little apart from some jewellery of sentimental value had gone missing, the old couple had taken it hard.

The day after the break-in, Shelley had stayed for a good hour and listened to their concerns. She hoped by the time she'd left they'd both felt reassured that the police were doing their best to find the culprit, and that the suggestions Shelley had made about improving their home security would make them safer in the future.

'So, how've you been, Elsie? Sleeping better?'

Sitting in Elsie's spick-and-span living

room with a cup of tea and a biscuit brought in on a tray by George, Shelley observed Elsie closely, as she stared down into her cup. George, clearly worried about his wife's listlessness, darted her an anxious look, before meeting Shelley's eyes pleadingly.

'I've told her they won't get in again, not with these new locks,' he said, 'but she won't take no notice.'

'I'm sure Elsie knows that deep down, George,' she said. 'But it's one thing knowing it and another entirely, when you wake in the night, not to let all those silly fears and worries flood in. I know I'm just the same.'

'George always thinks he can solve all my worries,' she said. 'And when he can't he gets annoyed with me.'

'I'm not annoyed with *you*, Elsie. It's those blighters that broke in I'm annoyed with! Turned you into a nervous wreck, they did. Making you imagine you can hear noises all the time.'

George had become so agitated that he spilled some tea into his saucer. Elsie berated him for his carelessness, showing a glimpse of her old spark.

'What noises, Elsie?' Shelley asked her.

'There are no noises,' George snapped, at the exact same moment as Elsie said, 'From next door.'

She could hear people moving about, she said, at odd times. And that was strange because the house had been empty for a couple of weeks, now.

'Foreign family. Don't ask me to pronounce the name,' George added. 'They've got a lad. Nice people. Quiet. Polite.'

'Not like some,' Elsie said meaningfully.

Shelley guessed she was referring to the Malarkeys, whom so far she'd not had the pleasure of meeting, although between them all they'd managed quite a portfolio of crimes of one sort or the other.

'Just up and offed,' George said. 'Not a word to say where they were going.'

'Probably just on holiday,' Shelley suggested. 'People don't feel the need to tell their neighbours their movements so much these days.'

'Not like the old days,' George agreed, offering to refill Shelley's cup with tea.

Shelley refused the refill but spent a few more minutes listening to George and Elsie's memories. She'd told them on her first visit that Burroway had once been her home, too, so their memories were always of interest to her.

It was with an invitation to get over to the community centre for a game of bingo and to catch up with friends who'd all been asking after them that Shelley finally made her exit.

Shelley's beat took her past her old school — Burroway Comp — an uninspiring building, which didn't seem to have changed at all since she'd been a pupil. School, with its ethos of conformity, had been hard for her. Ruby's unconventional looks and ways were different from those of all the other mothers on the estate. In their house, they had no TV, and the only music they listened to was of Ruby's choice — mostly bands she used to follow in her hippie heyday.

She grew used to being teased when

she turned up to school in her old-fashioned clothes, and to feeling left out of the conversation whenever it turned to the latest pop group. At the grand old age of forty-two, there were still times when she'd wake in the night in a cold sweat, after a particularly bad dream had brought her face to face with Josie Smith, the school bully, who'd had an awful lot of pleasure out of Shelley over the years.

It hadn't all been bad there, though, Shelley reminded herself, as she pedalled on, leaving the school behind her. After all, it had been at Burroway Comp that she'd met Glyn, her childhood sweetheart, whom she had eventually married.

Despite — or maybe because of — her unconventional upbringing, all she'd ever wanted was marriage and a family and she'd envisaged a long and happy future with Glyn. But, sadly, that was not to be. The last thing Glyn had said to her — before he slipped into the coma from which he was never again to emerge — was that she must always try to think of him as he'd been when they'd first met, and not how he became after the illness that was to kill him claimed his good looks and vitality.

This was harder on some days than others. But today, finding herself in such close proximity to the place they'd first met made it easier to keep that promise, and Shelley's heart lifted as happy memories flooded in. She'd been right to go for this job and, had he been alive, Glyn would have told her so, too. She knew he'd be so proud of her if he could see her now.

Shelley glanced at her watch. It was three o'clock. Debating whether or not to go back to her office, she decided that if PC Quinn had been able to introduce himself today, then he'd have done so before now. Her shift ended soon, but before she went home she thought she should pay a visit to this Mr Peter Farlow from the Allotment Society.

It was such a lovely day that she decided to cut through the park and take advantage of the fresh air. She spotted the small figure of a boy perched high up, at the top of the skateboarding slide. He looked very young to be there on his own

— she'd have said no more than eight or nine.

There was no adult around to supervise him, as far as Shelley could see, so she felt justified in approaching the boy. Dismounting her bike, she strolled towards him, calling out a friendly greeting. In her job, the softly-softly approach was crucial — the last thing she wanted was for him to run off before she'd had time to talk to him.

'Are you coming down?' she called. 'Or do you want me to come up?'

The boy shrugged by way of an answer and continued to look at his feet sticking out before him, clad in scruffy trainers.

'I'll come up, then, shall I?'

Taking his silence for encouragement, Shelley climbed the steps of the slide, grateful for her sturdy boots.

'Name's Shelley, by the way,' she said, as she climbed. 'What's yours?'

'Bradley,' the boy said.

'Have you got another name?'

'Malarkey.'

Shelley swallowed hard. Oh, well, it was only a matter of time and she'd rather make Bradley's acquaintance than his older brother's, who, by all accounts, was well on the way to following in his father's footsteps all the way to jail.

'Pleased to meet you, Bradley.'

Gingerly, Shelley sat herself down next to him at the top of the slide.

'No school today?'

'No. It's SATs.'

Assessment tests. Shelley had been through all that with Heather and was still going through it with Nathan. But didn't you have to be ten before you started those? Bradley was older than he looked, then.

'Have they let you out early?'

This conversation was a bit like mining coal with a teaspoon, Shelley thought, as Bradley shook his head again. He seemed to be struggling with something he wanted to say so, mustering all her patience, she waited.

'They don't want me there,' he said finally. 'So I stayed away. I'm staying away tomorrow, too. And the next day. Till they're done.'

Well, that was worth the wait, Shelley

decided. Now that she had a toehold in the conversation, she managed to get from him the reason why.

'Can't read or write proper, see,' he said. 'No point sitting staring at the wall, is there?'

Shelley's heart went out to the little boy, already a failure in his own eyes at such a tender age. If it were up to her she'd put an end to all tests. She'd been rubbish at them herself all the way through school, so she understood completely Bradley's reluctance to put himself through the torture of them. But playing truant was against the law and, as a PCSO, she couldn't turn a blind eye to it or she wouldn't be doing her job properly.

'How much longer were you thinking of staying here?' she asked. 'It's nearly home time now. What say I walk you to your house? Your mum'll be there, won't she?'

Fear crept over Bradley's face. 'My mam'll kill me,' he said.

'No, Bradley. If you're having problems at school, then she'll want to know about it,' she said, although she had no evidence to base this on at all. 'I know I would if it were my son.'

'No, not that,' he said. 'I mean she'll kill me if she thinks I'm bringing a policewoman home with me. She says we see enough of them in our house.'

At this, Shelley found it difficult to hold back a smile. In the end, by promising him he wasn't in any trouble with the police, she persuaded him to let her take him home, and one behind the other they made their slow way back down the slide and through the park to the exit and to Bradley's house.

'I live there,' he said, pointing. 'The house with the mattress and the old pram in the garden. The council were meant to come and take them away but me mam wouldn't pay the ten quid, so they left them.'

It didn't bode well, Shelley thought. To be honest, even if the council were to take the pram and mattress away, it wouldn't have made that much difference to the dilapidated, terraced house with its overgrown garden and cracked front path, which was even more of an eyesore because the other gardens in the street were all so well tended.

Nervously, she knocked on the door. It was flung open immediately by a woman about Shelley's height but twice as wide. From her fingers dangled a smouldering cigarette.

'This is all I need.' The woman raised her eyes heavenwards. 'Flamin' coppers on my doorstep.'

She glared at Bradley before yanking him over the threshold, demanding to know where he'd been, but continuing to rail at him even while he told her, thus making her none the wiser for all her questioning.

Shelley was sure she recognised Mrs Malarkey from somewhere but she couldn't think where. There was something about the anger that fizzed from her sturdy being like an electric charge, and the voice that grated like nails on a blackboard.

Suddenly, the penny dropped. The white-blonde hair with the dark roots and the extra two stones had confused her at first, but now she was sure. Mrs Malarkey was none other than Josie Smith, perpetrator of so many spiteful deeds when they'd been schoolgirls!

Temporarily done with Bradley, Josie turned her scowling face towards Shelley, who tensed up against attack, just as she used to in the old days. Any second now she was convinced she'd be recognised. But, after a brief, contemptuous flicker of the eyes, Josie simply returned her glare to Bradley while she thought up some fresh insults she could hurl upon him.

Could it be, Shelley wondered, that to a woman like Josie Malarkey, one person in uniform pretty much resembled another? When Josie, with one final glare, slammed the door, putting it squarely between them, Shelley realised her supposition had been correct. To Josie, Shelley was just one more faceless official. She'd had absolutely no idea who Shelley was at all and she for one had no intention of pointing out that, actually, she wasn't a police officer at all, but PCSO Shelley Lansdown. Née Bradshaw.

Still wobbly with the fear that had taken her over, Shelley remounted her bike and rode off in the direction of her office, then, as the adrenaline wore off, remembered where she'd been going before she'd spotted Bradley, and turned around, back towards the allotments.

A car drew up outside the gate as Shelley was locking her bike, and a very attractive woman, in her early fifties, dressed rather scantily for gardening, Shelley would have thought, got out to key in the code which would allow her inside.

'Come in with me if you like, love,' she said. 'Who are you after?'

'Peter Farlow. I just rang his mobile.'

'Pete? Not still going on about his precious spuds being nicked, is he, love him?'

Shelley recognised a Welsh accent from the way the woman spoke, and her rich, throaty chuckle strongly suggested that here was a woman who enjoyed life.

'Leave your bike. Hop in the car. Pete's plot's just next to mine.'

Gratefully, Shelley accepted the lift. The car smelled of the woman's perfume, musky and overpowering. She'd always imagined female allotment holders to eschew make-up, but Myra Roberts, as she'd introduced herself, was done up for a night on the town.

'He'll be disappointed they've only sent a PCSO and not M15,' she chuckled, as, after they'd driven a few yards, they pulled up by one of the plots.

'Here's Pete now,' she said.

A tall, burly man, much more suitably attired for gardening than Myra, even down to the wellies and flat cap, was waving his arms in an agitated manner and calling something out to them.

'My God, what's the matter with him?' Myra said.

He was right by the car now, tugging open the door on Myra's side, even before she'd put on the handbrake.

'Didn't I tell you this was getting serious? Well, come and look at this. Maybe you and your new German friend will believe me now.'

'What — what's happened?'

Shelley was out of the car in a flash. Myra, in her tight skirt, took longer to decant herself. She didn't think she imagined the look of longing in the allotment chairman's eyes as he took in Myra's long, tanned legs.

'I'm so sorry, Myra,' he said, in an accent Shelley recognised as coming from somewhere in Yorkshire. 'But they've had your artichokes now. Look! Every one!'

2

Shelley's running for the bus. Doesn't matter where it's heading. Ruby doesn't worry what time she gets home from school these days. Too busy making banners and protesting.

The stitch in her side is getting worse and she doesn't think she can keep up the pace. And then behind her footsteps ring out. A barrage of loud cries. *Oi, Shelley! Don't you know no one wears flares any more?* Laughter. *You won't need a tent next time you go off camping with your mam to Greenham Common!*

Oh! Please God! No! Pounding blood. Rasping breath. And hot. So hot. And then she trips. The pavement tilts towards her as she tumbles forward to meet it. Stupid clunky shoes. Stupid old woman's trousers. Sprawling on the ground, she knows it's all over for her. Artichokes come raining down on her head, their thistles stabbing her scalp and neck, and Josie Smith's accusation rings in her ears.

'This is sabotage, Shelley! You'll never get away with it!'

★ ★ ★

Shelley was awoken by the sound of her own yell of protest bubbling up from her throat.

She opened her eyes. Familiar curtains, the sun poking through where they didn't quite meet; her PCSO uniform hanging from the pelmet. Back in the real world. Safe. Another day, another challenge. One day in, and already she was letting the job get to her, Shelley thought, scrabbling in her pocket for her office key. She thought she'd left her Josie Smith nightmares behind along with her school bag, but their reunion yesterday had stirred everything up again, adding artichokes for good measure.

From the other side of the door came the sound of someone thumping a keyboard. Cautiously, she turned the handle and peeped inside. The police officer seated at her computer looked up, stopped typing and beckoned her in.

'PC Quinn?'

So this was the Community Beat Officer and her line manager at last, come to introduce himself. And help himself to her computer, too, from the look of things. They'd be working closely together so they'd better get on, but already she couldn't help feeling slightly resentful that he was sitting in *her* chair and logged in to *her* machine.

'You'll be Shelley,' he said, extending a hand she had to take two steps forward in order to reach. 'Excuse me if I don't get up but I'm not sure there's room for two fully grown adults to stand in this box room. I've been reading your reports,' he added. 'Very detailed.'

'Thank you.' Perhaps he was all right really.

'Actually, that's not really a compliment.'

She went back to her original opinion.

'This little — how shall I put it — love triangle down at the allotment.'

PC Quinn scratched his head, like he was looking for a good way to say something negative. Dark shadows beneath his eyes suggested a man on bad terms with a good night's sleep.

'I'm not sure, Shelley, that we need to get so involved with the private lives of members of the public. Not that it doesn't make very interesting reading.'

'I thought there might be trouble, sir. A woman called Myra Roberts accused Peter Farlow of pulling up all the artichokes that another member of the allotment society had been cultivating.'

'A Mr Rolf Scherfling.' He glanced down at her report once more. 'And did he, d'you think?'

'No, sir. I think — as I've said in my report — that Ms Roberts is playing one man off against another.'

Shelley felt aggrieved. Clearly Quinn thought she'd been wasting her time down at the allotment but it was solely down to her efforts that things hadn't escalated between Roberts — all pout and perfume; Farlow — big, solid and full of Yorkshire dourness; and the dapper, bearded Scherfling, who'd turned up later.

In a firm though conciliatory tone, Shelley had warned Myra that she couldn't go round accusing people of destroying someone's entire crop without proof. What would Mr Farlow's motives be in any case? She'd seen Farlow's face in the local paper many times. Chairman of Burroway Allotment Society, he was generally considered to be a force for good. Myra's accusation seemed just plain silly to her. Myra had tossed her head at Shelley's words and accused Farlow of being jealous.

'Rolf grows specialist crops from seed, and all organically, too. Those artichokes would have won gold at next month's Flower and Produce Show without a doubt. All Pete's got to show for his efforts are his boring old marrows.' She spat out the last word venomously.

'That's ridiculous,' Farlow countered. 'I told you, I came in here half an hour ago, and when I saw all this I rang Rolf straight away.'

'That proves nothing,' Myra said

darkly. To Shelley, she said: 'Rolf was going to feed me one of those artichokes, you know. Tomorrow. At his house. A taste of heaven, he said.'

A gruesome image of Myra, melted butter running down her chin, being fed artichokes from an invisible hand, popped into Shelley's head. As Myra stared wistfully at the spot where the artichokes used to be, Shelley noticed Farlow's equally wistful glance towards Myra. To Shelley, it was obvious that Farlow's feelings for Myra were as strong as Myra's were for Rolf. But would he stoop so low as to destroy his rival's crop? This man had soil under his fingernails. He probably read seed catalogues in bed. Gardeners loved plants. They didn't destroy them. But what if a woman was involved? Even then it seemed pretty far-fetched to Shelley and certainly not something a Yorkshireman would do.

And where did Rolf fit into all this? she wondered. The crunch of tyres on gravel, the rumbling of an engine and the creak of a handbrake had alerted them all to the fact that a car had pulled up outside the gate and someone was getting out. If this was Rolf, she was about to find out.

Everyone's eyes had turned towards the gate. Shelley's heart was in her mouth. Was Scherfling under the same impression as herself that vandals had caused this destruction, or had Myra already called him and filled his head with her suspicions? And if so, would he come tearing inside any second now and, without bothering to ask any questions, simply knock Farlow's head off?

She needn't have worried. Once inside the gates, Scherfling didn't even see Farlow but headed straight for his plot, where he hopped balletically from row to row, occasionally falling to his knees to inspect the destruction, muttering in German and shaking his head solemnly, as yet more damage presented itself. She could have sworn she saw a tear glistening on his cheek and felt slightly embarrassed by such a performance. Myra, wringing her hands in sympathy, seemed, on the contrary, to be lapping it up.

'If there's anything I can do,' Farlow

said, clearly as embarrassed by Scherfling's performance as she was.

Myra, with a mean glance at Farlow, drew herself up to say something, but Shelley shot her a warning look. If she were about to launch another attack on Farlow then she was going to have to suffer the consequences, the look said. For a moment, Shelley felt herself rather enjoying the small amount of power invested in her by her uniform and badge. Next time she got into a confrontation with Josie Smith, she would remember that she had the law on her side!

'No, no, my friend,' Scherfling said, in reply to Farlow's offer. 'You did everything by ringing me. I thank you. But as far as these are concerned — ' he waved his hand at the decimated plot — 'there is nothing to be done.'

He'd left soon after, saying he'd be back later to tidy up but that right now he had to get back to work. Shelley heard Myra ask him *when, later.* She was no Poirot but a row of peas could have worked out what she was getting at. She wanted to be there to help him when he

101

returned, and no doubt to spread more weed killer on Peter Farlow's reputation.

'This bit about Myra Roberts being the type to enjoy two men brawling over her,' PC Quinn said, bringing her back to the present with a jolt. 'I'm not sure that would stand up in a court of law, Shelley.'

Shelley muttered something about it just being an opinion and he could scrub it if he wanted.

'That's exactly what I intend doing,' he said, handing her the report. 'Or rather, what *you'll* be doing when I've gone. Our job is to record what we see, not what we feel. We're not social workers, Shelley, though God knows sometimes it feels like it.'

After PC Quinn's departure, Shelley felt uneasy. She'd never had a line manager before. When she'd left school she'd worked briefly in an office and had a boss, big, blustery Mr McGee who breezed in and out but rarely impacted on the lowly work that Shelley had been engaged to do. Soon after, she'd got married and pregnant — or, more truthfully, pregnant and married — and that had been the end of her working career.

She'd hoped, when she started this job, that there'd be people working alongside her she'd be able to make friends with — share a joke and a bit of banter. But from what she'd seen so far, PC Quinn didn't do banter. He hadn't even revealed his first name. Was he to be PC Quinn for ever? One day in and already she'd got on the wrong side of him.

He wasn't the only person she'd got on the wrong side of either, today. Both Heather and Nathan had been sulking when she'd left this morning — although for different reasons.

The morning routine had begun well enough — no one fighting for the bathroom or hogging all the breakfast cereal. Shelley had even made them laugh, retelling her dream, particularly the bit about the artichokes.

'In real life, Josie was much more subtle,' Shelley had told them. 'Little digs with the point of a compass, drawing pins on the seat — that kind of thing.'

'And you say this Josie Smith lives on

your beat?' Heather asked.

'That's right. Of course, there's much more of her these days and she's changed her name to Malarkey, but she'll always be Josie Smith to me.'

It was when Nathan mentioned that he knew a Malarkey — a boy called Kevin from school — that things began to go downhill. There was a programme on TV he and Kevin were obsessed with, he said — Shelley had seen it once or twice; a host of good-looking people running around on a desert island chasing an inexplicable plot — and they'd chat about it sometimes while they were waiting for the teacher.

'Is Kevin Malarkey in your sets?' a surprised Shelley had asked.

'For Maths and Science,' Nathan had replied. 'Why?'

'Because Mum's a snob,' Heather chipped in. 'She doesn't like the idea of them letting a Malarkey into the top sets with her precious son!'

Shelley had denied this vociferously. She was just surprised, that was all, that Josie Smith had managed to produce a clever child. She tried to make light of it by adding that she shouldn't have been really because, after all, she'd managed the same feat herself and she'd failed practically every exam she'd ever taken.

But her joke had backfired big style. She'd said *child* and not *children* and Heather — always prickly where her academic abilities were in question — had taken it as an insult. Shelley had insisted she hadn't meant it so, but it was too late to take it back. The damage was done.

The fact was, though, Heather *didn't* have her brother's brains, which was why Shelley had suggested a vocational course at college for her. She seemed happy enough now, with her new friends. Maybe it was time to stop feeling guilty for perhaps not encouraging Heather through school as much as she could have. But that was the dreadful time when she'd been consumed with Glyn's worsening illness. Heather was good at making her feel guilty, even after all this time. If they'd been offering GCSEs in it, she'd have come out with a starred A.

Perhaps it should have come as no surprise when Heather responded as she did when Shelley reminded her she'd be working late, so Heather was in charge till she came home.

'Mum, I'm at college, now,' Heather had protested. 'Anyway, I'm going out straight after my last session and I won't be back till late.'

Maybe, in hindsight, Shelley had been wrong to explode. But she'd thought she'd got a firm promise from her daughter that on weekday evenings she'd be there to make Nathan's tea before he went off to whichever of the many after school activities he happened to be involved in.

The bickering between them had gone back and forth, with nothing being resolved. Shelley had accused Heather of dropping all her old friends in favour of this new set. Heather had denied it before going on to accuse Shelley of mollycoddling Nathan, who was perfectly capable of feeding himself and putting a load of washing on. Shelley said it wasn't mollycoddling — she just didn't want her son being a latchkey kid.

'Then you shouldn't be going to work till Nathan's eighteen, in that case,' Heather had snarled, triumphant in her logic. 'Because he'll still be your little boy even then, won't he?'

Shelley had said nothing, though she'd felt like saying plenty. Heather had always had a sharp tongue, and while for the most part she tolerated her little brother and even, occasionally, admitted to quite liking him, if ever the opportunity arose to point out just how much she thought Shelley favoured him above her, then, like this morning, she grabbed it with both hands.

Of course, it was all nonsense. Shelley loved both her children equally. But if you've got a choice between a hedgehog and fluffy kitten to stroke, it's not that difficult to choose between them.

Nathan, surprisingly, sided with Heather. He didn't want her to feel obliged to come running back straight from college just to open a tin of soup he was perfectly capable of opening himself, he said, but Shelley wasn't happy and said so.

Nathan was a scatterbrain. Any chore you asked him to do he'd do it, without the heavy sigh that usually accompanied the same request made to his sister. But often he'd forget, halfway through, just what, exactly, it was that he'd been asked to do. His head was full of so much stuff that it was easy to imagine coming back to an empty house with the front door left open and the TV set missing, or a kitchen full of smoke because he'd got distracted by something he'd been reading and forgotten to turn the grill off.

'You'll have to go to your gran's,' she insisted. 'She can make you tea on the days I can't be here.'

So that had led to her falling out with Nathan. Gran's houseboat was too far away to get to from school and, besides, she was a worse cook than he was. That was one thing they both agreed on, but Shelley, running late, decided not to go there. The one thing about Nathan was that he wasn't the rebellious type. He'd go to Ruby's for tea just to keep on the right side of her, she was pretty sure. She was just sorry that Heather had let her down.

Shelley's day, after a muddled beginning, quickly began to take shape once she'd substituted what PC Quinn had implied as her purple prose for something a bit less imaginative. A visit to Burroway Primary School, where she had an interesting chat about little Bradley Malarkey's literacy problems — his mother, apparently, had taken not the slightest interest in the material about remedial reading classes that they'd sent home — took up most of her morning and the afternoon was taken up with routine patrol.

Her mobile rang just as she was turning the corner into Keats Drive, where the Butterworths lived. Hopping down from her bike to take the call, it was George Butterworth's anxious voice she heard.

He didn't want to call the police because he wasn't sure if a crime had been committed or not, so he thought he'd ring Shelley, who'd probably know what to do better than a policeman anyway.

Shelley was intrigued and more than a little flattered. She suspected it was something concerning Elsie — maybe her nerves were still getting to her after the break-in and George thought it needed a woman's touch.

'You're in luck, George,' she said. 'I'm outside your house right now.'

His hand trembled as he shook hers and ushered her inside and through to the sitting room, making Shelley fear that something was badly wrong.

Elsie sat in her usual chair, in a voluminous, floral wraparound overall. She must have been about the same age as her own mother but, apart from the white hair, their style was very different. Ruby loved colour and wouldn't wear an apron on principle. *A symbol of oppression,* she called it — alongside stiletto heels and girdles. But for Elsie, an excellent cook and baker, her apron was a badge of honour.

Elsie attempted to struggle to her feet and was clearly relieved when Shelley gestured for her to stay seated.

'It's OK, Elsie,' she said. 'Just tell me

what the matter is and I'll see if I can help.'

It was a strange tale and Shelley wouldn't have believed it if, five minutes later, she hadn't seen the evidence, or rather lack of it — herself. It was tempting, now she'd heard the story twice from start to finish, to put everything down to absent-mindedness. After all, Elsie had been under some strain since thieves had broken into her house and she was the first to admit she hadn't slept well since then.

'I'd just baked my usual batch of scones and set them out to cool, like I always do,' she began. 'George had popped out to take his library books back, so I thought I'd just have time to put a bit of washing out before he got back then we could have our tea and scones together.'

'It's our routine, see,' George put in.

'So there I was in the back garden, pegging out, and then the phone rang. I thought it might be George, that he'd had an accident or something, so I ran in to answer it, not thinking for a minute I'd left the door wide open behind me.'

She shot Shelley a guilty look, as if she fully expected to be reprimanded for her carelessness, but Shelley simply smiled and patted Elsie's hand.

'Go on,' she said.

'The phone's through there, by the front door, as you know,' she continued, casting a glance in that direction. 'Anyway, when I picked it up, there was nobody on the other end. I waited a bit for it to ring again, but it didn't, so I decided to finish my pegging out. And it was when I went through to the kitchen again that I saw what had happened to my scones.'

'And what was that, Elsie?'

'They'd gone. Every last one of them!'

Shelley darted a puzzled look at George. All sorts of things went through her head. Did George think that Elsie was having some sort of crisis, mixing up her days so that in actual fact she hadn't done any baking at all? But the first thing to greet Shelley, even before George had said hello, had been the delicious smell of home baking — Elsie couldn't have made that up.

First artichokes disappearing from the allotment and now Elsie's home-made scones. What on earth was happening on the Burroway Estate?

3

If she hadn't sniffed the evidence herself, Shelley would have drawn the conclusion that poor Elsie Butterworth had simply lost the plot — but what about the crumbs scattered around the cooling rack? That was forensic evidence. And it would last a great deal longer than the doubtless already faded scent of home-baked scones that had greeted Shelley's nostrils as an anxious George Butterworth opened the door to her earlier today.

It was definitely a police matter, she'd told George and Elsie. If someone was entering their house uninvited and taking their things, these were criminal acts that deserved to be investigated.

'Do you think this is the same person who broke in before, Shelley?' Elsie asked as she saw Shelley out.

Shelley didn't know what to say. What, she wondered, would make Elsie feel less at risk of it happening again? The fact was that, however she answered, the result would be the same. Elsie would feel that she and her husband, old and therefore vulnerable, had become a target for villains, and that the police, who'd so far got nowhere solving the first crime, had bigger fish to fry. In the end she'd been non-committal, dressing up meaningless phrases in the pretty wrapping of upbeat buzzwords. It was with a heavy heart that she said goodbye.

Now she was back in her office, writing up her report. PC Quinn, her line manager, wouldn't be able to fault her unembellished style this time, she decided, as she placed the final full stop. Previously he'd complained of too much irrelevant detail in her descriptions.

It was time to go home. She'd done all she could for the Butterworths — the rest was up to the police. She'd have liked to stay and help, but she had a family to see to. Tomorrow she'd make the Butterworths her priority, with a visit to the allotment next. Once more, little Bradley Malarkey and his educational problems would have to go to the bottom of the list — though she guessed that both at school and at home he was well used to that. If things were disappearing from the allotment as well as from the Butterworths, though, maybe there was a connection, and the sooner she sniffed it out the better. She certainly didn't believe Myra Roberts' theory that Pete Farlow, in a jealous rage, had pulled up Rolf Scherfling's artichokes — organically grown from seed, at that — because Myra fancied them more than she fancied Farlow's carrots.

Shelley grinned to herself as she recalled a desolate Myra regretting that the evening she and Scherfling had planned — in which he'd promised to cook these same artichokes — would now never take place. One glance in the direction of the dour Yorkshireman had revealed how hard it must have been for him to shut out the image of the sultry Myra, butter dripping down her chin, being fed exotic vegetables by her German seducer — and his arch-rival.

Shelley's radio suddenly crackled into life.

'*Disturbance at Waterside. Woman threatening to drop some young lad's motorbike ignition key over the side of her houseboat. Anyone deal? He says she's barking, so go easy when you get there!*'

Shelley's grin faded. Yanking her coat off the hook, she hurriedly thrust her arms through the sleeves. Ruby. It could only be Ruby. What on earth had she done now? If it's not one thing, she mused, as she mounted her bike and headed out towards Waterside, it's your mother. Shelley arrived just in time to see the back of Ruby's white head as she was being driven away in a police car. Through the crowd — Ruby's neighbours, she presumed, all waving and cheering in support — she glimpsed a familiar tall, lanky figure. Nathan, schoolbag slung over his shoulder, slouched towards her. If only he could have been somewhere else, his body language screamed, then that was where he'd rather be.

'Mum! Do you know what's going on?'

Suddenly remembering he was meant to be having tea with Ruby, which explained his presence at Waterside, Shelley rushed over. Her first instinct was to hurl herself at him and hug him tight, but that was something she rarely did these days, and never in public.

'I haven't a clue, Nathan, but I'm guessing your gran's been up to her old tricks of righting wrongs again,' she said, grim-faced. 'Wait there and I'll see what I can find out.'

Some of the onlookers shrank back at the sight of a uniform, but one or two recognised Shelley as Ruby's daughter and were more than happy to fill her in on the events of the afternoon — although, one shaven-headed, multi-tattooed and pierced resident of indeterminate age confided, the real story had started a while ago, when the clocks had gone back and the lighter evenings had first begun.

'Drove us nuts, they did,' he said. 'Lads. About his age.'

The man gestured towards Nathan, whose neck sank even further into his shoulders with embarrassment.

'Up and down. Revving their engines, churning up the ground.'

'Didn't you call the police?'

The man rolled his eyes. That'd be a no, then, Shelley decided with a frisson of irritation. It irked her just how many down on Waterside, like her mother, felt that the police were suspicious of their alternative lifestyle and could never be expected to be sympathetic towards it.

'Your mother likes to take the law into her own hands,' the man replied.

'Tell me about it.'

Shelley couldn't be sure how much was true and how much embellishment, but gradually she was able to patch together the gist of the story. An hour later, down at the station, her mother filled in the missing pieces.

As a favour to her uniform, Shelley had been allowed down to the 'soft' interview room where Ruby — free to leave at last — was fastidiously sipping tea from a polystyrene mug and grimacing at the contents. A weary duty solicitor, putting away his papers, gave Shelley a weak smile as she entered. She felt sorry for him. He was probably wishing for a nice easy case — a mass murderer, for instance — anything but this wild, white-haired old lady, clearly possessed of the combined zeal of Joan of Arc and Margaret Thatcher.

Although she'd been charged with theft and — unless a miracle happened — was going to have to appear in court, the prospect had done nothing to dampen Ruby's defiant mood. When Shelley took her to task about what she'd done, she simply said that the day she allowed herself to be bullied by youths, like the ones who'd tried to bully her, would be the day she took to her bed and stayed there for good.

'And don't think I'm expecting any favours just because you're wearing a police uniform, Starling,' Ruby added. 'I'm looking forward to my day in court.'

Shelley winced at the pet name she hated. 'I bet you are,' she mused. There was nothing her mother loved more than a bit of limelight. As a campaigner back in the heady days of Women's Lib, then later at Greenham Common, she'd been arrested more times than Shelley cared to remember. She reminded her mother that now the process of law was in place there was absolutely nothing she could do to get her out of this, even if she wanted to. And to be honest, Shelley wasn't sure she did.

She was still trying to get her self-possession back after the humiliation she'd suffered walking the gauntlet of police officers earlier, many of whom had witnessed Ruby being brought in. Having to claim the 'feisty geriatric' as her mother and putting up with their good-humoured wisecracks hadn't been easy.

'That's all you're worried about, isn't it? How me getting arrested reflects on you! Nothing changes, Shelley, does it?'

Shelley was livid. Her mother was wrong. This wasn't why she was angry with her at all.

'If only you'd come to me,' she said. 'I could have talked to the lad, shown him we were on to him and his gang. They'd have moved on and left you in peace if they thought they had the police breathing down their necks.'

Ruby sighed. 'We don't all have your faith in the long arm of the law down on Waterside,' she said. 'I wasn't just acting for myself, you know, when I removed that ignition key from that young man's bike.'

'I'm sure you weren't, Mum.'

She predicted the phrase 'standing up for what you think is right' — hidden for so long at the back of a drawer — was due to be taken out, dusted and given an airing.

'You have to stand up for what you think is right in this world, Shelley. It's not right to go round intimidating people on their own property just because you're young and strong and angry, and you can.'

Bingo! You had to admire Ruby's bravery, though some would call it foolhardiness — the arresting officer upstairs, for example. Shelley's thoughts skipped briefly to Elsie Butterworth, who'd grown so timid over the past couple of weeks. How different the two older women were in their attitudes!

'Nathan was coming to visit. Didn't you see him? What sort of example is it for a young lad to see his granny being bustled away into the back of a police car?'

Said like that, Shelley could almost see the funny side. She suppressed a smile. As much as she admired her mother's nerve, she had to make her see that the law applied just as much to her as it did to anyone else.

'I'd rather you didn't use the word 'granny' if you don't mind, Shelley.' Ruby shuddered. 'What did he want, anyway? He doesn't usually come round after school.'

Shelley explained how Heather had let her down and there was no one at home to keep an eye on him, so sending him round to Ruby's for tea had been the only choice available to her.

'You spoil that boy, Shelley.'

Shelley's good humour quickly faded.

'He's only young. I don't like him coming home to an empty house. I was always there for Heather when she came home from school.'

She didn't know why she'd brought up Heather's name. Maybe it was as a justification, to show she didn't favour one over the other, whatever Heather — and by the sound if it her own mother, too — thought.

'Well, just remember that he's your son, and not Heather's responsibility. This new job of yours is a good opportunity to release those apron strings.'

'I came here to see if you'd like to spend the night at my place,' Shelley replied stiffly, 'not to be given advice on how to bring up my children.'

In the end, Ruby refused her offer, insisting her friends would be waiting for her back at Waterside — which suited Shelley just fine. One more person to squabble with over the bathroom in the morning was all she needed.

Next day, Shelley was in a tetchy mood. She'd fallen asleep in the chair some time after eleven and woken at midnight to no sign of Heather. Dragging herself up to bed, she'd undressed and climbed wearily under the duvet, but had been unable to go back to sleep. When Heather finally arrived home, she'd wondered about going downstairs to confront her, but thought better of it and turned over.

This morning Heather had overslept and blamed Shelley for letting her sleep in, which led to Shelley reacting in exactly the way she'd hoped to avoid. Now Heather wasn't speaking to her again.

At work, there was an e-mail waiting for her from PC Quinn, asking her to print off half a dozen police posters and deliver them to the local shops. A small gang of youths, harmless enough at the moment, were beginning to annoy not only the shopkeepers but also customers. The posters were official police warnings stating that the youths could be subject to prosecution if they continued to gather outside the shops in such numbers. It was hoped, so PC Quinn's e-mail read, that the wording on the posters would be strong enough to stop trouble before it began — particularly with the school holidays beginning any day now.

Shelley resisted the urge to ignore the e-mail. She had her own 'to-do' list. She felt bad about Bradley Malarkey. Had he taken any more time off school? It had occurred to her that Bradley might have a problem with dyslexia. She'd even thought about picking up some leaflets about it to pass on to Josie, but knowing Josie she'd see this as busy-bodying. Far better to reach her through a third party, which was how the idea of visiting the school came to her. Now she was going to have to leave it for another day.

Then there was the possible connection between events at the allotment and at the Butterworths' — not to mention the noises from the house next door. Her scepticism over what Elsie had insisted she'd heard wasn't nearly so strong now she'd witnessed for herself the disappearing scones. She cursed PC Quinn for his interference in her day, but nonetheless dutifully made the photocopies and headed for Broad Street, where the row of shops that serviced the Burroway Estate were situated. If all she did was to drop off a poster and kept the chat to a minimum, she could be back on track in no time.

Broad Street was quiet at this time of day. A sullen-looking youth, leaning against a lamppost opposite the news-agent's, showed his disdain for her uniform by sneering as she went inside. She'd seen him around — one more hoodie she didn't think she'd ever be able to bring herself to hug — but had never had occasion to speak to him, thank God. Not that she was going to let his insolent posture affect her treatment of him. Crossing the threshold, she turned her attention to the shop assistant, guardedly watching the youth through the window from behind the cover of a magazine stand.

When Shelley realised who the assistant was she did a double-take. So this was what the lovely Myra Roberts did with her day when she wasn't breaking hearts and driving grown men to deeds of horticultural violence. Myra seemed equally surprised to see Shelley, and more than a little relieved.

'Just keeping an eye on that one,' she said, moving away from the window and taking her seat behind the till. 'Wouldn't trust him as far as I could throw him.'

'Is there anything I should know?'

'Where do I start? Just Darren Malarkey being Darren Malarkey.'

Another Malarkey. She might have guessed. It was more than likely he was one of the youths the shopkeepers had complained about. Shelley handed Myra a poster and advised her to put it up in the window where it could clearly be seen.

'Let's hope that makes him think twice before he starts anything,' Myra said, in her fruity Welsh accent.

She looked as if she were about to launch into a tirade against youth in general, but Shelley, mindful of time, had her own agenda.

'How's everything down at the allotment? Those two men still fighting over you?'

Myra patted her magnificent hair, all thoughts of Darren Malarkey suddenly wiped away now she was back on her favourite subject — herself. What time did she get up in the morning, Shelley wondered, to look as good as this?

'Trouble with that Pete Farlow is that he's a jealous man. There's nothing between Rolf and me. I was just trying to make him feel welcome — him being a foreigner and all. But Pete? Well! Thinks he's got some sort of claim on me. And that's why he did what he did to Rolf's artichokes. He must have overheard him inviting me over to taste them.'

So Myra was still sticking to her claim. Well, now wasn't the time to disprove it — but maybe later.

What happened next was confusing. A scuffle of feet, followed by a loud roar from outside, and an irate figure, waving his hands in the air, yelling, 'Stop, thief!' at the top of his lungs. Shelley dashed outside, already on her radio, calling for a police officer to attend the scene immediately, with Myra following hot on her heels.

'It's Darren,' she yelled. 'Look! There he is! What's he been up to now? And that poor man wringing his hands is Mr Patel from the off-licence!'

Shelley followed Darren's progress down the street, as he weaved between pedestrians, who jumped aside nervously to let him pass. She could have run after him, but she'd never have caught him. Besides, she had no powers of arrest and on no account was she expected to tackle a member of the public.

'Little perisher! Only had my back turned for a minute and he's pinched a bottle of my best Scotch!'

Mr Patel, clearly agitated, was breathing fast and shaking with fury. Shelley asked Myra to bring him a chair and a glass of water, which she quickly did.

'I've radioed in a description, sir,' Shelley said. 'They'll be on to him soon, don't worry.'

But she hadn't bargained on how soon Darren Malarkey would be captured. It wasn't a uniformed officer who was to be thanked for his swift reaction, however, but a member of the public. Shelley, more concerned with calming down Mr Patel, missed the exact moment that the youth was brought down but, at the sound of another cry, found her attention momentarily diverted away from him. Further down the road, on the other side of the street, Darren was sprawled on the ground, holding his ankle and howling with pain, the contents of the smashed bottle of whisky running in rivulets around him.

Above him, waving his walking stick triumphantly, was none other than George Butterworth, with an equally triumphant Elsie by his side, gazing up at her husband in adoration. Shelley sprinted across the road towards them. The smell of whisky from the bottle was all pervading, but stronger than that was the powerful scent of victory that — in the space of a minute — had added to his stature and taken years off George.

'I got him, Shelley!' George yelled, still waving his stick around for all to see. 'I got the little blighter!'

When it was all over and the police car had taken Darren away, Shelley, Myra, the Butterworths and Mr Patel retired to the back of the newsagent's for a well-deserved cup of tea, business being temporarily suspended on both premises.

Myra's nerves seemed to have got the better of her after all the excitement and she couldn't seem to stop talking. In the space of two minutes, the gaps in Shelley's knowledge about the Malarkeys were completely filled. Poor Josie had her work cut out trying to keep her elder son in order while his dad was inside, according to Myra. Luckily for her, the other sons were so different. Bradley was a sweetheart and Kevin one of the most helpful boys you'd ever meet. Why, only last week he was running errands for the neighbours and often stopped to help her push her wheelbarrow back from the allotment when it was full of produce. You'd never catch Kevin up to Darren's tricks, marching into the shop bold as brass, complaining that his mum's daily paper hadn't been delivered and refusing to pay his bill because of it.

'I delivered it through his door myself,' an irate Myra said. 'That Josie just doesn't want to cough up what she owes, that's all!'

'You're probably right, Myra,' Shelley agreed.

'Funny thing is, though . . . ' Myra hesitated, as if she didn't quite know how

132

to phrase what she had to say.

'Go on,' Shelley prompted.

'It's odd, that's all. I've known him years and would never have said Darren was an accomplished liar. You can always tell when he lies — eyes all over the place — but when he swore blind for the third time they'd never had their papers this week? Well . . . I believed him.'

Myra bit her lip, as if it pained her to say it.

'So if I'm telling the truth, and he's telling the truth — who's been nicking their papers every morning, Shelley?'

4

'You again? What's so interesting about my family that you can't keep away?'

Josie Malarkey née Smith had taken an age to answer the door. Shelley cast her eye over the faded pink stained candlewick dressing-gown that was obviously Josie's daytime ensemble of choice.

'You might want to get out of that and into something less comfortable.' Shelley's tone suggested she was not to be messed with, Josie or no Josie. 'I'm afraid I'm here with some bad news.'

The two women had been in the B stream together. Neither of them had learned much, but one subject Josie had excelled in was how to deny culpability in whatever misdemeanour she'd been found accused of. When Shelley informed her that Darren had been arrested for shoplifting, it was clear that Josie had lost nothing of this skill. She'd just transferred her defence from herself to her son.

According to his mother, Darren was just a boy who'd gone through life being misunderstood. Blamed for this; blamed for that. That cow at the newsagent's, Myra Roberts, for example, insisting she'd been delivering their papers, when Josie would be prepared to swear on her own deathbed that she hadn't had so much as a peep at her favourite red top for a week at least! Then threatening all sorts when Josie had refused to pay up! That was why she'd sent Darren round — to reason with the Welsh dragon.

Why was it no one ever believed them when they told the truth? They'd had no papers, *end of*, but was anybody listening? If he'd ended up running off with a bottle of whisky it would have been *her* fault for riling him, not Darren's. Anyway, that Mr Patel had never liked Darren ever since the time he'd once left his shop accidentally without paying for some cigarettes and sweets. On and on she went, like Vicky Pollard's mum. Her final remark had left Shelley open-mouthed with amazement.

'It was just unfortunate that he'd been

deprived of a strong role model at a critical point in his adolescence,' she quoted, back at her office, to an equally disbelieving PC Quinn, her taciturn line manager.

'That would be the role model currently serving time, then, would it? Her old man.' PC Quinn shook his head in amazement. 'You've got to admire the woman's nerve.'

'She's one of those women who just can't seem to see reason where her kids are concerned. There's just no getting near her.'

It was a relief to be having a conversation with PC Quinn in which they were on the same wavelength — for now at least.

'Don't try,' he said. 'Just do your job and keep your distance.'

Shelley turned over his words. What was it with this man? *Keep your distance. Don't get involved. Remember you're not a social worker.* He was such a cold fish. Policing was just a job for him, not a vocation. That was the impression he gave her, at least. She'd have liked to bring up the subject of little Bradley and his reading problems. Despite being so busy, she'd finally managed to squeeze in a visit to the school and had had quite a chat with Bradley's teacher, who'd been horrified to learn the real reason for him taking the day off, which in no way tallied with the tummy ache excuse on the note he'd brought from home the following day.

The teacher, Miss Smart, a patient woman with a kind but careworn face, had told Shelley that she'd asked his mother to come in twice already this term and been ignored on both occasions. They wanted to test Bradley for dyslexia but it meant taking him off site and without her permission they couldn't go through with it. Shelley had volunteered to bring the subject up next time she bumped into Josie. But this last encounter had hardly been the right time. Shelley didn't really want to go round there again, but her conscience was bugging her and she suspected it would only be a matter of time before she heeded its nagging. There was something about little

Bradley that had tugged at her heart-strings and it just wasn't letting go.

'Heard about your mum, by the way.'

'What have you heard, exactly?' Shelley glared at him.

Now it was PC Quinn's turn to look uncomfortable.

'Oh — nothing, really. Just — you know. About the arrest and everything.'

Attempting to cut through the frost that had suddenly settled between them, he added, 'She's a feisty one by all accounts.'

Shelley glared some more. Wrong word choice, buster, her expression said.

'I expect it's all round the borough. But there's no need to be delicate. Feisty's good, but I bet they've been using other adjectives down at the nick to describe what a fruitcake the old girl is.' Her irony was intended. To his credit, PC Quinn looked deeply embarrassed.

'Don't worry,' she snapped. 'I'm used to people laughing about my mother behind my back. I've had it all my life.'

'If you want, I'll chase it up. Find out if they're going to prosecute.'

Shelley shook her head vigorously, annoyed by his conciliatory tone. She didn't need anyone to feel sorry for her. 'No thanks. My mother wouldn't thank you for giving her a way out. What she did — taking that key and threatening to drop it into the river unless those lads promised to take their bikes away for good and leave the residents in peace — she did to make a point.'

'The point being?'

'That you have to stand up to yob culture and be seen to stand up to it.'

'All very well — until somebody hospitalises you for your pains.'

PC Quinn's words seemed to choke him and his complexion turned a deep red. What was he so furious about? Shelley wondered. The frost had turned to ice all of a sudden and this time it wasn't of her making. Whatever rapport they'd had at the start of their conversation had suddenly disappeared. The next hour was spent in an uncomfortable silence, with both of them answering calls, writing up reports and other mundane tasks. It was with relief that

Shelley finally made her escape and headed out to patrol her beat.

What was going on at the allotment today? she wondered, putting PC Quinn right out of her mind. She had the code to get in from Pete Farlow, the Chairman of Burroway Allotment Society. *Come and have a look round any time,* he'd said on the phone after their last meeting. *I'll feel safer if I think the place is under surveillance for at least part of the day.* He'd joked that she might even get lucky and catch whoever had really taken Scherfling's would-be prize organic artichokes in the act of committing yet another crime. If he were the culprit, as Myra Roberts still insisted, would he be so welcoming of a police presence?

It occurred to Shelley, as she punched in the numbers and silently let herself into the allotment, that Pete Farlow might even have suspicions of his own. If he was there now, perhaps they could spend some time discussing them.

But the allotment was deserted as far as she could see. At this time of year everything was growing in abundance. Shelley skirted the edges of those plots near the entrance, admiring the produce on offer. How tempting it would be to grab a handful of those luscious-looking raspberries over there, or to snaffle up a lettuce and some ripe red tomatoes to make a salad later. Not that she ever would, of course. But maybe she'd have a word with Farlow and ask him what the chances were of getting a plot here. This stuff had to be better for you than those salad bags and tired vegetables on offer at the supermarket, and just think of the saving she'd make.

She caught a sudden glimpse of a figure in the distance. Wasn't that Scherfling's plot? And wasn't that Scherfling himself, tending his plants? She wondered about going over to say hello, but thought better of it. Gardeners were like anglers. They got so wrapped up in the moment that any interruption could easily be met with an unwelcome glare. Glyn had been an angler. He could sit for hours by a riverbank just gazing out at the water, so she knew what she was talking about.

What would he have said to a plot on this allotment? Shelley wondered. The two of them — Derby and Joan — harvesting carrots and potatoes for the winter, side by side and thoroughly contented. Pity that would never be.

Funny, she could go for weeks without thinking of Glyn, but then one day, when she least expected it, there he'd be before her again, as sharp and clear and solid as if he were still alive. Would it be always so, she wondered, or would there come a time, when she was old and grey and walked with a stick, that she'd be unable to remember his face and that infectious laugh of his?

Blinking away the wistful thought, she switched her concentration back to the distant figure. Scherfling was busy, obviously. Whatever he was doing he appeared to be in a big hurry. Up and down the rows of tomatoes he went, occasionally looking over his shoulder. It was all very suspicious. Shelley crept nearer. He seemed to be carrying something in his hand. A bottle or spray of some sort that he was squirting liberally at the fruit. Did organic gardeners spray tomatoes? Shelley didn't think so, though she was no Carol Klein.

Just as she'd decided to turn back and let herself out of the gate, having decided she was wasting her time here, she glimpsed another figure — taller, sturdier and equally familiar — hurtling towards Scherfling. It was Pete Farlow and he looked furious. For a moment Shelley stood slack-jawed, unable to do anything but watch as Farlow snatched the spray from Scherfling's hand and pushed him down on to the ground, where the smaller man lay cowering in surrender.

Shelley finally roused herself and sprinted towards the two men, both of whom by this time were yelling, though Scherfling was still on the ground. But Shelley's lungs were as powerful as the next man's and, when she ordered Pete Farlow to stand away from Scherfling, both men fell silent — Farlow taking a few steps back, his expression sheepish now, and Scherfling looking up at Shelley in gratitude for coming to his rescue.

'Are you going to tell me what's going

on?' Shelley demanded.

Scherfling struggled to his feet. He endeavoured to look nonchalant, casually dusting the soil from his trousers as if he'd gone down on the ground of his own accord. His smile was only for Shelley — very charming, she thought — and very false.

Pete Farlow held out the plastic spray that he'd snatched from Scherfling's hand and thrust it at Shelley. She managed to read the words: *destroys all garden pests chemically* before he removed it from her vision again.

'Evidence!' Farlow said. 'We'll see what the Committee has to say about this. I'll be calling an extraordinary meeting urgently.'

'What's going on? Pete? Rolf?'

Myra, in bright pink shorts and with a cleavage you could hide a crop of radishes in, was teetering up the path towards them in strappy sandals. To give him credit, Shelley thought, Peter didn't look particularly triumphant. In fact, he made a half-hearted attempt to hide the evidence behind his back, but Myra spotted it and wrestled it from him. She scrutinised the writing on the bottle then, with a furrowed brow, cast a puzzled glance from Farlow to Scherfling and then back again. Was neither of these men going to explain? Shelley cleared her throat.

'I think you'll find that Mr Scherfling has been telling lies about his crops being organic,' she said. 'And Mr Farlow here has just caught him in the act.'

Myra looked with disbelief at Farlow. Shelley recognised that look. Before Myra could follow up with her interpretation of what really must have happened, Shelley let it be known that she'd witnessed the entire proceedings herself.

'Is this true, Rolf?'

Scherfling raised his hands in surrender.

'It's just a spray,' he said. 'What harm can it do?'

Pete and Myra locked eyes, both aghast. Shelley understood their horror at Scherfling's words. He'd deceived the Committee and lied to Myra for his own ends. What was worse was that he hadn't understood the importance of honour. This little allotment society was many years old with a history of fair play and integrity, and Scherfling, with his cavalier attitude to the truth, had demonstrated a blatant disregard for common values.

Would Myra realise her mistake at falling for the wrong man and try to make it up with Pete? Would Scherfling be thrown out of the society on his ear? And if so, would that mean there was a plot going begging that could have Shelley's name on it? Whatever was going to come of it all, it didn't need the presence of a PCSO. She was glad she'd been around to witness Scherfling's downfall, and she'd be more than happy if Myra Roberts finally looked further than the end of her nose and saw that not only was Pete Farlow a good man but he was besotted by her. But it was time for her to leave them to it.

★ ★ ★

The rest of the week passed without event — apart from the welcome news that

Darren Malarkey had confessed to breaking into the Butterworths and stealing Elsie's precious jewellery. He categorically denied having anything to do with taking scones from their kitchen, however, but the feeling down at the police station was that it was only a matter of time before he'd put his hand up to that too — and that sooner or later he'd stop whingeing on about the papers his poor mother was having to pay for that hadn't even been delivered.

Shelley learned all this from PC Quinn on Friday afternoon just as she was about to go off duty for the weekend. He seemed to be trying to make it up to her for his earlier display of temper. The reason for his outburst still puzzled her but Shelley decided to give him the benefit of the doubt.

He was intriguing though — an able-bodied man in his prime who could have been out there on the front line, yet he'd chosen to become a community beat officer instead — a role he really didn't seem fitted for at all, in Shelley's view. When she'd told him, for instance, that on Sunday she would be visiting the Butterworths for a celebration tea, he'd given her that look again. *Why are you getting involved with these people?* it said. *They're not your friends.*

'Why don't you Google him?' Ruby suggested, when Shelley mentioned she was curious about his choice of profession.

She was visiting for the day because the new computer had arrived and Nathan had promised her a lesson on how to use the Internet when he'd finally set it up. A quick learner, Ruby had already caught on to the idea of Googling and was working through everyone she knew or ever had known, in order to discover more about them. For today, at least, the incident with the biker and the keys was completely off-limits.

Shelley, dressed in a new cornflower blue wraparound dress that Ruby said matched her eyes and enhanced her waist, was ready to set off for the Butterworths' party. Elsie had invited the rest of the family too, but Shelley had declined for them. Nothing would get

Nathan away from his new toy and she suspected her mother would have nothing to say to either of the Butterworths after the first five minutes.

As for Heather, Shelley wasn't even going to go there. She'd been late in again last night and had only just surfaced from her bed. When Shelley had asked her — as non-confrontationally as she could — what she'd be doing for the rest of the day, she'd muttered something about a project for college tomorrow.

The properties and composition of hair, she'd replied dully, when Shelley asked what her project was about. To her comment that it sounded interesting, all Heather said was *not really but she had no choice in the matter as she was studying hairdressing*. Shelley put her bad mood down to a hangover, but, as she left the house for the Butterworths, she couldn't shake off the niggling feeling that maybe there was something more.

But it was a lovely day and nothing was going to spoil it for her. It seemed strange to be strolling down Keats Drive, where the Butterworths lived, in a summer dress and sandals, a handbag on her wrist instead of a radio strapped to her chest.

'Doesn't she look lovely, George?' A beaming Elsie said as she opened the door to welcome Shelley inside.

'And you look grand yourself, Elsie,' Shelley said. 'Nice pearls.'

Elsie was dressed for the occasion, too, in a cotton dress instead of her usual baggy top and trousers, although she'd clearly felt unable to discard her ubiquitous apron. Round her neck she wore a string of pearls — the necklace that Darren Malarkey had filched from her jewellery box along with her other trinkets. At Shelley's compliment, she put her hand to her throat and flushed slightly. She was a shy young girl again, Shelley decided, entertaining in her own house and very much in love with her strong, handsome husband, who'd single-handedly brought down a villain.

George was out the back, Elsie said — they thought they'd have tea outside, it being such a lovely day. The summers were so short these days that it seemed a pity not to take advantage of good weather. Shelley allowed Elsie's happy chatter to wash over her. It was such a change from the desperate silence that had so often met her when she'd visited on previous occasions and it reminded her just why she'd wanted to take this job in the first place.

Two hours had passed and Shelley — full to bursting — was insisting that it really was time for her to head back home or her kids would think she'd run away.

'I'll just visit the little girls' room first, if that's OK, Elsie,' she said.

The bathroom window opened outwards and Shelley could see right into the back garden of the house next door. The Abolas, the family who lived there, still hadn't returned from their mystery travels, she'd been told but, fortunately, neither had those noises that Elsie had reported coming from the house. Maybe it really had all been in Elsie's head — brought on by her nerves after the break-in.

But, just as she turned her head away from the window, a figure came out of the back door, arms full to bursting with an assortment of household wares — Shelley distinguished a pan, some clothes, a bucket filled with things she couldn't see. It was a boy, Nathan's age — at first glance it could even have been Nathan, so strong was the resemblance and so similar the clothes.

The young boy glanced up and saw Shelley watching him. As if a starting pistol had been shot, he was suddenly off — down the path and struggling, hands full, to open the gate to the cobbled back passage. Shelley, just as quickly, was down the stairs and out the back door in seconds, leaving the Butterworths open-mouthed behind her. She hurtled down the garden path, cursing her sandals and, wrenching open the gate, she was soon almost upon her quarry. For if she was at a disadvantage in her flimsy footwear, he was even more so. Making the mistake of looking behind him, he failed to spot the dustbin that tripped him and brought him to his knees.

'Stay down!' Shelley cried. 'I'm police. You've been caught red-handed stealing from next door. Now tell me your name.'

The Butterworths, who'd followed Shelley at a more leisurely pace, had finally caught up with her.

'That's Kevin Malarkey,' Elsie said. 'He's a friend of Kofi from next door. What are you doing with Kofi's football boots, Kevin? And that top — I'd recognise that print anywhere. It's Kofi Abola's mum's. One of her African outfits.'

Not another Malarkey! Shelley groaned inwardly. But this was the nice one. Everybody said so. Nathan's friend too! What was he doing pilfering from the empty house next door?

'I'm saying nothing,' the boy said firmly. 'I reserve the right to remain silent.'

5

'You heard what Shelley said,' Elsie told Kevin. 'She doesn't want the police involved. If you can just explain what you're up to with someone else's belongings, then maybe we can sort it all out without them having to know anything about it.'

Shelley was impressed with Elsie's no-nonsense manner, and told Kevin, 'You're not a thief. You're a good boy. That's all I've heard from those who know you. So why have you been taking things from the Abolas? And not just today but on other occasions, too? Don't deny it, because Elsie here has heard someone walking about in there.'

Kevin's face was inscrutable, though the constant crossing and uncrossing of his lanky legs suggested he wasn't as confident as he'd have liked them to think.

'D'you know anything about my

scones, by the way?' Elsie suddenly blurted out. She'd previously complained to Shelley about a batch of freshly-baked scones going missing from her kitchen.

'What is this — *Twenty Questions?*' Kevin snarled.

Whatever Kevin was up to wasn't for gain, Shelley was convinced. But why wouldn't he stand up for himself and at least lie a bit? Then she might have a reason to dislike him. OK, so if he didn't respond to threats from the police, maybe it was time to roll out the big guns.

'What's your mother going to say when she finds out another of her sons has been involved in theft, Kevin?'

'She'll get over it. She married me dad, after all, so she's had the time to.'

Over his head, Shelley and Elsie exchanged looks of concern. Kevin's determination not to co-operate was unshakeable. It seemed he'd be arrested rather than explain just what he was doing with Mrs Abola's floor-length dress, among other items. Even Kofi's football boots were at least three sizes too small, judging by the size of Kevin's great big feet.

'I'm going to give you a chance, Kevin,' Shelley said, wondering if it might cost her her job. 'The things you took from next door I'm going to put back. Key, please.'

She thrust her hand under Kevin's nose peremptorily and waited as he searched his jeans pockets one by one for the key. Shelley resisted a smile at her own cunning. So, he hadn't broken in — which was a good thing. Now, had he stolen the key or did he have a right to it? Had Kofi given it to him? Or Kofi's parents? And if so, why?

'And now I'm going to trust you to go home and explain to your mum just what you've been up to.'

Kevin raised his eyes heavenwards at this.

'Then tomorrow — first day of the school holidays, so you have no excuse not to be there — I'll be round to hear the truth. If you still refuse to talk, I'll have no alternative but to report it.'

It was dusk when Shelley got back

home. The long walk gave her plenty of thinking time, but before finally setting off, she'd popped next door and let herself in, to see what she could see.

Downstairs all was neat and tidy. If the Abolas had left in a hurry, there was no evidence of it. Maybe it had been Kevin who'd washed the dishes, neatly stacked on the draining board. Upstairs, the beds had been stripped. Drawers and wardrobes were still stuffed with unseasonably warm clothes but there was no evidence of summer clothing. Neither could she find any towels or blankets in the airing cupboard and the bathroom was bare of toiletries. What could it all mean?

Ruby, Shelley's mum, was climbing into a cab that had arrived to take her back to her houseboat by the time Shelley — still puzzling over what to do about Kevin — reached home. She'd been learning how to use the Internet on Nathan's new computer.

'Darling! At last!'

Shelley apologised for being such a long time, but Ruby brushed her words aside.

'Never mind me, dear. It's Heather you need to worry about. She's not happy on her hairdressing course and she thinks she's stuck with it. It's up to you to tell her different.'

Shelley was stung by Ruby's words. Heather was *her* daughter, not Ruby's. If she wasn't happy, why hadn't she told her before, instead of keeping it to herself, then blurting it out to Ruby? Then she forced herself to take a step back and look at the situation from Heather's point of view. Maybe she *had* told Shelley that she was unhappy. Not in words but in deeds — staying out late; sleeping in at the weekend; keeping any contact with her mother to a bare minimum for weeks now.

'Don't look so sad. It's not your fault. It's just the way of things. Glyn's illness and everything after. You had a lot on your plate. Understandably, it was easier to let her get on with things — we females are good at coping.'

'Does she really think I don't care about her?' Shelley felt a welter of emotions — exasperation being right up there with dismay and guilt.

'Of course she doesn't. But maybe there was a time — you know, when Glyn was dying — when she didn't feel she could bother you.'

The cab driver turned his ignition key, impatient to leave.

'Go on, Mum,' Shelley said. 'Go home. I'll talk to Heather.'

'Remember, you're a great mum,' Ruby called out, through her open window, as the cab sped away. 'Don't be too hard on yourself.'

Shelley took a deep breath as she let herself inside. It was a long time since she'd had a heart-to-heart with Heather. Too long. Ruby was right. It had been easier to take her word — that everything was fine — at face value. A habit she'd got into years before when life with an ailing husband and two children had been such a struggle that, at times, she'd had little time or energy left to devote to helping Heather with her schoolwork. And then it was too late. By that time Heather had earned the label — *not really the bookish type*. How easy it was to judge other mothers — Josie Malarkey, for instance — when just as much fault could be laid at her own door, she thought, getting out her key.

Immediately she crossed the threshold, Nathan launched himself at her, waving a printout off the computer.

'Wait till you see this, Mum! You'll never believe it!'

'Not just now, love,' Shelley said with a weary smile. 'I have to talk to Heather.'

'But Mum! It's about — ' 'Nathan! It'll wait. Where's your sister?'

It was fortunate that Nathan was blessed with more than his fair share of sensitivity. She was upstairs in her room, he said. And she'd been crying.

'Thanks, love. Tell me all about it tomorrow,' she called out behind her, as she dashed upstairs. 'Right now, Heather and me have got something to sort out.'

Heather was already in her pyjamas when Shelley, at Heather's brusque 'come in', put her head round the door.

'Your brother says you've been crying and your gran says you're unhappy at college. So, here I am. I've got all night.

Talk to me about it, Heather.'

It was a real temptation to ask why on earth she'd not said something sooner — after all, a whole academic year had passed since she'd first embarked on her hairdressing course. But instinct told her to hold her tongue. It took time but Heather, perhaps sensing there'd be no interruptions, began to open up. She thought it'd be a laugh, she said, and besides, with her rotten GCSEs, what else could she have done? But the subject didn't interest her and she'd quickly grown out of the friendship groups she'd fallen into at the start of the year.

'They were a laugh at first. But, honestly, Mum, you wouldn't believe some of them. It's all make-up and clothes and boys, boys, boys; 'Does he like me? Does this suit me?''

'Does my bum look big in this?'

It was a relief to see the smile on Heather's face at this.

'I wish I'd worked harder at school. If I'd got better GCSEs, I could have done A-levels.'

'Is that what you want?'

Heather shrugged. 'I don't know. I just want to do something in my life that makes a difference. Social work. Teaching, maybe.'

Making a difference. Exactly like Shelley had always longed to do. And Ruby too, albeit in her own anarchic way. And so began the most honest conversation Shelley had ever had with her daughter. About being a mother, and making mistakes and wishing you could start again because nothing was more important to her than Heather's happiness.

'It wasn't your fault, Mum,' Heather said. 'It can't have been easy for you — with Dad. Ruby made me realise that.'

Shelley thought of Ruby fondly. However much they rubbed each other up the wrong way, her mother had always been her staunch supporter. Just like Shelley was Ruby's — though it often pained her.

'We'll go into college and talk to someone who can advise you about resitting your GCSEs,' Shelley said. 'Then we'll let the Hairdressing Department know you won't be coming back next year.'

Shelley slept easier than she'd done in a long time that night. Next morning, waiting for the kettle to boil, her eyes alighted on the printout that Nathan had been waving at her. It was an article from a national newspaper, dated roughly two years previously. Quickly, she read it through.

PC Guy Quinn left hospital yesterday, walking unaided for the first time since being attacked by a gang of would-be robbers who had broken into a computer store in Finsbury Park, London. Quinn, 40, a divorced man with more than twenty years' exemplary service in the Metropolitan Police, was answering a call to check on the store, after a passer-by had called the police with suspicions of a break-in.

The gang set about him, wielding cricket bats, and Quinn sustained multiple injuries, including two broken arms and several broken ribs. But even under attack, Quinn bravely managed to hold them off and made the call for back-up, a call which undoubtedly saved his life.

The intruders fled the scene empty-handed and were quickly caught.

Asked yesterday if he would be going back to front-line policing, PC Quinn offered no comment.

Shelley, shocked by what she'd read, thought how quickly and stupidly she'd pre-judged PC Quinn — or Guy, as she'd just now discovered he was called. What a dreadful experience it must have been! Had he decided, even while in hospital, that never again would he put his life on the line? Did he apply for the position of Community Beat Officer, in a small town far away from London, because he'd lost his confidence on the beat? If so, who could possibly blame him?

She guessed Guy Quinn's 'it's just a job' attitude and his obvious disapproval of Shelley's approach to it must have stemmed from this one incident. Twenty years' exemplary service in the Met. He'd been a brilliant copper once, then. She should remember that. One thing was certain — she'd be treating him with a great deal more respect from now on.

'You've read it, then?' Nathan stood in

the doorway, hair tousled and face creased with sleep. 'Cool bloke.'

He dragged himself over to the bread bin and flipped it open. Until now, she'd never have said the word cool applied remotely to PC Quinn, but now — well, she had to agree.

'Super-cool,' she said. 'With knobs on.'

Changing the subject, she asked Nathan his plans for the day.

His blank expression showed her he had none.

'Well, in that case, you can give me a hand.'

Nathan groaned. 'Not cleaning the bathroom,' he protested.

'No, not cleaning the bathroom — though now you mention it, maybe it wouldn't do it any harm. Tell me all you know about Kevin Malarkey.'

'Kev? What do you want to know about him for? What's he done?'

Shelley described her encounter with Kevin the day before and her visit to the Abolas' empty house.

'It looks like he's been taking things — not just from the Abolas but from

165

other neighbours, too.'

The newspaper delivery that had gone astray, that Darren Malarkey was still insisting had nothing to do with him — was Kevin responsible for that, too? she wondered.

'Kevin's not a thief, Mum.' Nathan was indignant.

'Well, what is he then? A kidnapper? Where are the neighbours, Nathan? They've not been seen for a fortnight or more.'

Nathan frowned. He seemed to be remembering something or working something out. At last he spoke.

'I don't know if this is anything to do with it, but Kevin usually has school dinners.'

Shelley nodded.

'Free ones. Some idiots laugh at him as if being poor's a cause for merriment.'

Shelley loved her son. She couldn't help it.

'Go on,' she said.

'Well — he stopped having them a bit since. Round about the time Kofi stopped coming to school.'

'Right.'

Maybe there was a connection but, whatever it was, she wasn't getting it just yet. She asked Nathan what sort of boy Kofi was. Nathan was vague. He was OK, was all he could come up with. Did Kevin like him? Were they friends? Sort of, he supposed. Shelley guessed that was all she was going to get. If this were Heather she were talking to, she'd have chapter and verse about exactly the kind of relationship the two friends had — but that was the difference between boys and girls for you.

'Then there's this other thing. Seemed funny at the time, because Kevin never speaks up in R.E. No one does. But last week he had a right go at somebody for saying there were too many immigrants in this country and there should be tighter controls. He said that people like Kofi's family, for instance — who'd sought asylum to escape terrible persecution back in their own country — should have the right to stay in the UK. In fact, he said he'd rather they lived here than some of the scroungers that were born here.'

'Is that really what he said? People like Kofi's family?'

Nathan and Shelley stared at each other. She couldn't have said for certain which of the two of them worked it out sooner. But they both agreed that Kevin Malarkey must be protecting Kofi and his family from the authorities, who must be threatening to repatriate them.

★ ★ ★

It had been a fight to stop Nathan following her to Josie's but she had to be firm. This was police business. Now she stood in Josie's kitchen, more determined than ever to get to the bottom of the mystery.

'He hasn't told *me* anything, so you can stop looking at me like that,' Josie said. 'None of my kids ever do.'

Maybe before last night's discussion with Heather, Shelley would have sneered at this. But not now. 'That's kids for you,' she said instead. 'Mine are exactly the same.' She turned to Kevin.

'I know you're protecting Kofi's family,

Kevin,' she said. 'I've worked it out. If only you'd tell me what's going on then maybe we can help them.'

'How? By putting the immigration officers on to them and getting them deported?'

Kevin looked suddenly defeated. He slumped back in his chair, as if he'd realised it was just too hard to keep his secret any longer. In a monotone, avoiding Shelley's eyes and ignoring interruptions from his mother, he finally came out with the whole story.

Three weeks ago, a worried Kofi had arrived at school with news that a letter from the immigration office had arrived that morning, stating that the family was in breach of regulations and they were going to have to return to the African country from where they'd arrived in Britain eight years previously. Kevin, through contacts he'd found on the Internet, had found a safe house for them. They'd fled, empty-handed, and since then Kevin had done his best to keep them in food and clothing, any way he could.

It took everything Shelley had to persuade Kevin that the family would have to give themselves up. Only then could their case be heard. In the end, albeit reluctantly, he agreed.

'You should be proud of this one, Josie,' Shelley said when she called in again the following day to inform Kevin that the family — discovered managing as best they could in a ramshackle caravan in the depths of Blessingham Wood, two miles away — were being fairly treated by the authorities and there was no need for him to worry. 'He's got a good heart.'

Although Josie's reply to this was that Kevin had better start saving up because he owed her a fortune for the food he'd taken off her, not to mention for the newspapers she'd never received, the pride in her eyes as she heard praise heaped on her son was unmistakable.

* * *

A few weeks later, Shelley, in trackie bottoms and an old T-shirt, was mowing the lawn, reflecting on how well every-thing had turned out in the end. The Abolas were back in their own house, after the authorities had admitted that a mistake had been made sending out the letter, and their right to remain in this country had been reinstated.

Kevin had agreed to help the Butter-worths in their garden, in return for the scones he'd taken. The business of the artichokes was cleared up, too, when he revealed that Myra had paid him for helping her with ferrying her heavy gardening tools back from the allotment last winter by giving him some seeds of his own.

Josie, taking the law into her own hands as usual, had decided that lettuces and tomatoes were one thing but courgettes and artichokes were a mystery to her. She'd passed these particular packets to her neighbour, Rolf Scherfling, in return for a packet of fags. So really, in helping himself to a few artichokes, it could have been argued that he was only taking back his own property — and Shelley for one had no intentions of disputing his logic.

The final thing to lighten Shelley's load was that she'd managed to persuade Josie that having young Bradley Malarkey tested for dyslexia was not a way to 'slap a label on him' — but a way of making sure he finally got the best help available in the classroom.

Grinning to herself, she happened to glance up as PC Quinn came striding over the lawn towards her, calling to her something she couldn't hear. She quickly switched off the mower. What on earth could he want? And her in her Sunday scruffs, too!

'Your daughter let me in,' he said. 'Hope you don't mind me coming round on your day off but I've got some news you might want to hear.'

The case against Ruby had been thrown out, he said. A few weeks previously, much to Shelley's embarrassment, Ruby had been arrested for stealing a biker's ignition key. He'd been disturbing her neighbours and Ruby wasn't standing for it any more. However, the young menace involved was now in hospital, PC Quinn said. In a bad way, but he'd come round eventually. The bike he'd been riding had been stolen — something only discovered when it was found wrapped round a tree with him on the ground beside it.

'That's good news,' Shelley said. 'Not for him, of course. He's still some mother's son.'

'You've a good heart, Shelley,' PC Quinn replied.

Shelley flushed. 'Why didn't he wait till tomorrow to tell me this?' she wondered. 'Why today?' As if reading her mind, he said, 'You and me — I think we've got off to a bad start. I came round because — well — I thought it might be something to celebrate over a drink in a pub.'

'You want me to ring my mother so she can join us?'

Now it was his turn to look flustered.

'Only joking,' she said.

She was playing for time but didn't know how to reply. By saying she didn't think it was appropriate, perhaps? Or that she was in the middle of her chores? Or that the children wouldn't approve if their mother went on a date? She thought about telling him she was a widow. But then something nudged her inside. A voice. Glyn's voice, as she remembered it. Strong and resonant and full of love.

'Say yes,' it said.

Closing Time

1

DC Myra McAllister thrived on challenge and that was official — set out in black and white on the many excellent references that had secured her transfer to Brising nick.

In her time as a serving officer back at Unwin Street, she'd worked her way up through the ranks. She'd talked down at least half a dozen distraught members of the public from various high altitudes, and put away several dangerous criminals for a long time, despite the machinations of their wily lawyers.

So, resettling at the other end of the country to be closer to her father should be a piece of cake. Or that's what she'd been telling herself for the past month, at least. Dad had had a stroke that had affected his sight and balance. Whatever he insisted to the contrary, it would have been a foolhardy gesture, once he'd been discharged from hospital, to allow him to

177

move back to the house he'd lived in all his married life — the house in which Myra herself had been raised — and go back to looking after himself.

But moving him away from Brising and ensconcing him in her flat would have been even crazier. Myra loved her dad, but she loved her independence more. OK, she wasn't particularly proud of the admission, but there was no point pretending — either to herself or to her father — that she was any different now to the teenage girl who'd gleefully shut the door on her home at eighteen to join the police force without so much as a backward glance of remorse. In fact, her dad would be so shocked if she suddenly morphed into a 'dutiful daughter', that he'd probably have another stroke.

To Myra's relief, he'd been more open to her suggestion of the retirement home than she'd anticipated. 'You don't want me under your feet and, to be honest, I wouldn't want it, neither,' he'd said, when she'd first, very cautiously, mooted the idea.

If those words had emanated from her

mother's lips, she'd have crept away from his bedside feeling so guilty that she'd have tossed Cedarwood Hall's glossy brochure into the nearest convenient bin on her way out of the ward, and immediately started phoning round for quotes from removal companies.

Avoiding saying what she meant had been her mother's greatest talent, Myra sometimes thought. But Dad was a plain-speaking man. If he said he didn't want something, then Myra could be sure he was expressing his true feelings. So it was settled.

Except she was his only living relative, and she'd never forgive herself if he didn't feel happy at Cedarwood Hall, despite his protestations that he was sure he'd love it. When she put in for the transfer, some of her colleagues back at Unwin Street told her that they thought she'd lost her marbles. Others said she was a saint. She was definitely no saint, though she wasn't sure if she could vouch for the where-abouts of her marbles. But the fact was she really felt she had no choice. She was duty-bound to keep an eye on Dad, and if that meant leaving behind her friends and workmates, and her lovely flat, then so be it.

There were other flats, and colleagues and friends, too, just waiting for her in Brising. All it took was for her to make the effort. Less than a month in, and she had the flat and the colleagues — and tonight she was working on the friends bit. Which is where her biggest challenge lay since she'd arrived in Brising.

It was eight-fifteen on a Saturday night and here she was, dressed — utterly ridiculously, in her opinion — as a WPC circa 1962, complete with headgear and footwear so unflattering it was a wonder any girl in her right mind back in those days had ever even considered the police force as a career. If there was any way of wriggling out of tonight's party gracefully, then she would.

All day she'd been praying for a call from the station — something *huge* like a major drug bust or even a mad axeman on the loose — anything to rescue her from this act of folly.

But the only person to ring her had

been Dad, asking her if she'd put a bet on for him and, unless she got a call from the station within the next half-hour, she knew she had as little chance of slipping her neck from this particular noose as a condemned man on the gallows.

'Sixties bash at The Guildhall,' WPC Ann Harris had remarked, spotting Myra by the canteen noticeboard one lunch-time a couple of weeks back.

Myra hadn't even noticed the poster WPC Harris was referring to. She'd been engrossed in quite another notice at the time. A rather dog-eared, faded one, asking for a volunteer for the role of police rep on a committee being set up to improve relations between Brising's trav-elling community and its townsfolk.

Reading it, Myra couldn't help wonder-ing what the lack of enthusiastic volunteers for this particular role suggested about Brising Central nick, and hoped it didn't mean what she thought it did. Namely that any attempt at building bridges between the two parties was a lost cause, because prejudice on both sides was too firmly entrenched.

She knew Brising's attitudes to the travellers of old — in fact, she could still, if pressed, recite a list of alternative, derisory names for the word traveller, all of which had been common currency throughout her childhood and, for all she knew, still were.

No one in Brising in those days would have poured a pan of cold water over a traveller if they'd been on fire, though they were happy enough to take advantage of the fairground rides and sideshows the travellers laid on for their entertainment.

From the state of the yellowing notice on the board, people weren't exactly clamouring to be part of this new committee. She didn't blame them either. The word bargepole flashed into her head.

Ann Harris's voice broke into her thoughts. 'You must come! It'll be a laugh, she said. Adding, at Myra's puzzled expression, 'This Sixties thing. At the Guildhall.'

Myra located the poster at last, read it and grimaced. It was all right for Ann

Harris to cavort around on the dance floor in a miniskirt, but Myra had been a founder member of the Sixties and she didn't think her impression of Cathy McGowan would go down as well in 2009 as it had first time round.

Though, thinking about it, she'd been rather a chubby teenager. It was more than likely she'd impressed no one with her moves but had simply, with the insouciance of youth, bopped and boogied herself into believing that she was more than a match for anyone on the floor.

'It's for charity,' Ann went on. 'And it's a great way of meeting people when you're new. And if you don't want to wear a mini, I can put you in touch with Trish Morley. She's managed to get hold of a job lot of old WPC uniforms for the — er — older lady, from somewhere or other. Friend in the BBC props department or something, so I heard . . . '

The poor girl tailed off miserably, crimson with embarrassment. Myra felt sorry for her. This was the first overture of real friendship she'd had since arriving at her desk the previous day, though everyone had been polite enough. And she wasn't complaining — it was early days, after all. She hated parties but she'd go — for all the very good reasons Ann had given.

'You've just sold it to me,' she said, to Ann's obvious delight. 'And less of the older lady, if you please!'

Ann apologised, mortified.

'Ancient's more the word for it,' Myra joked.

Me and my big mouth, she sighed, as catching sight of her reflection in the living room mirror back in her flat, she rummaged in her make-up bag for blusher. She needed something to brighten her face, that was for sure. Thinking back, it had been the prospect of wearing navy blue for the rest of her life that had decided her that she was more suited to CID than Uniform. Best decision of her life.

She decided on a glass of red wine for Dutch courage before setting off. For all her superior rank, she was still the new girl on the block. Everyone at Brising

Central went back years — it was plain to see from the banter that swung back and forth all day long.

All she could do was watch from the sidelines and try to work out who mattered most and who least, who was to be feared and who pitied. It pretty much felt like she was the one at the bottom of the heap right now. She didn't even know where the paper clips were kept.

The day Ann Harris had sold her the ticket to the Sixties party coincided with the day Myra found herself being volunteered for a place on the very committee she'd been reading about, and had decided she didn't want anything to do with.

Maybe she only had herself to blame — she'd sounded so enthusiastic about familiarising herself with Brising's policing issues when the Super popped in to see how she was doing. He must have thought Christmas and his birthday had arrived at the same time, judging from the way his face lit up as she spoke.

'Funny you should mention it,' he'd said, 'but tomorrow evening is the first meeting of this new traveller/townsfolk initiative and we still don't have a rep. I was going to go along myself, but now I've heard what you have to say, Myra, well, I think you'd be perfect for the role. A new broom and all that — untarnished with all the history that the rest of us have had to live through. What do you say?'

Idiot! She applied rather too much lipstick, then dabbed at it furiously with a tissue. In the background her radio was playing. Normally, she was a Radio 4 girl, but since the move, she'd taken to tuning in to Radio Brising in the hope that it might acclimatise her to the local scene. Although she was Brising born and bred, she hadn't really been back, except for the odd visit, since she was in her mid-twenties.

In those days, there'd been a dance hall, three cinemas, a swimming pool and a thriving open-air market. Only one cinema remained now, the open-air market had been replaced by one of the big-name supermarkets, and the dance hall had been bulldozed to make way for a multi-storey car park.

Very different times indeed. But one thing remained unchanged. Which was that the local community were still just as polarised in their opinion of the travellers as they'd been when Myra was growing up.

She nearly fell out of her chair when she heard the voice of Stuart Weeks, Brising's MP, coming from the radio. She turned up the volume to hear him more clearly. Hearing him speak again took her right back to last week's fraught meeting. Especially as he seemed to be repeating, practically word for word, the very same remarks.

'The idea that the taxpayers of Brising should willingly fund the expansion of a permanent site for these travellers, in the current economic climate, is simply risible,' he said silkily, in a way that was intended to make the listener feel curmudgeonly if he or she disagreed. 'Running water and electricity! And the right to call Old Common their own piece of land to hand down to future generations! No, no, no.'

Mouthing a silent apology to the half

dozen or so assembled men and women around the table, Myra, made late by the detour she'd taken to call in on her father, had scrambled her way over to the last available seat in the meeting room at the town hall. She'd always hated being the centre of attention and en route had prayed and prayed she might be allowed to slip into the room unnoticed.

Fortunately, her luck was in — thanks to the man holding the floor, who was clearly revelling having everyone's eyes on him. She recognised Stuart Weeks MP, straight away. Hardly surprising, since whenever she opened the local paper, there he was, grinning out at her.

It might have been a coup for the committee to have someone like Weeks come to address them but, personally, she'd long since stopped being impressed by politicians.

How could they ever be trusted to put the country's long-term future before their own desperate desire to be re-elected? As far as she was concerned, it was a joke.

It seemed she wasn't the only one to be unimpressed. The rather dishevelled woman sitting beside her, who'd clearly begun her art work as soon as the meeting had been convened and had already covered an entire side of an A4 piece of paper with doodles, furiously added another, scouring lines deeply into the page.

She seemed to crackle with barely suppressed rage. Myra put it down to the synthetic material of the crumpled suit she was wearing.

'I really must object,' she squeaked. 'Everyone knows there's a local election coming up soon. The travellers don't have the luxury of a vote, do they, Mr Weeks?'

There was a ripple of dismay around the room at this remark. It seemed obvious to Myra that Stuart Weeks was a lot more popular among the present company than the woman who'd just spoken.

The straight-backed man on Myra's other side leaned back in his chair, nodded in agreement, but said nothing. From his unconventional appearance, Myra decided, he was probably the only traveller present. Unless they'd all taken to wearing shiny navy-blue suits like Weeks'.

'Please address your remarks to the chair, Ms Potter,' the weary-faced Chairman said.

Myra scanned her agenda and quickly located Audrey Potter's name. *Health Visitor with special responsibility for the traveller community*, she read. The man in the chair went under the name of Councillor Bill Rigg. Myra had looked him up already and discovered that his ward backed directly onto the common where the travellers had set up home.

No medals for guessing which side he was on, then. Like Weeks, his loyalties were bound to lie with his constituents, who were worried what effect a permanent site for the travellers in Brising might have on their house prices.

Not that Myra blamed them. She'd lay odds that even the most liberal-minded person present — Ms Audrey Potter, for instance — would soon become a NIMBY if a band of happy travellers decided to set up camp in her backyard.

'These travellers have been moved from

pillar to post for years now, never allowed to stay in one place for any length of time and with no proper facilities, such as running water or electricity. Is it any surprise that the mortality rate within the community is so high?'

Audrey Potter's voice was rising to a squeal, the more agitated she became. Around the table, the expressions on the faces of the other members of the committee were hard to read, but Myra guessed that for most people present, Ms Potter's worthiness made them less, rather than more sympathetic to her cause.

Someone called out that she should stick to the agenda, and another gave a cry of 'hear, hear'. People began muttering and grumbling, and it was beginning to look as if the chairman had lost his grip on proceedings. Only Stuart Weeks remained silent, a smug reminder, Myra decided, that in the midst of insanity, he remained an oasis of rational calm.

A large woman with ornate hair and too much make-up, who was taking the minutes, whispered something in the chairman's ear. A tea break — the straw the English love to cling to in times of stress — was suggested and seized upon by everyone present, and the atmosphere relaxed.

Myra didn't want tea. She just wanted to get on with it. Her agenda gave the impression that still to come was the lack of a noticeable police presence in Bill Rigg's ward. If she was about to be thrown to the lions, she'd prefer to get the savaging over with sooner, rather than later.

Only she and her neighbour on the other side remained seated during the break. He introduced himself as Joseph Keogh, the travellers' representative.

'You have an ally in Ms Potter at least,' she said.

'One ally in a roomful of people is something, I suppose,' he replied. 'Though I'd rather she were a bit less . . . ' He struggled to find the word.

'Strident?'

'Exactly. That's a good word.'

When he smiled, Myra caught the flash of a gold tooth. How old was this man?

she wondered. He could have been anywhere between forty and sixty-five. With his flamboyant clothes and his abundance of silver-streaked hair, it was impossible to tell.

'Maybe if you were to take to the floor yourself,' she said tentatively, 'some of the attention would shift from her to you.'

He had a pleasant voice, with a trace of an Irish accent. The committee were bound to take to him much more readily than the expert on traveller health, Audrey Potter, she thought.

He shook his head. 'Words are not my thing, Detective Constable. I get tongue-tied in front of people like this. Besides, they already know what they think of us travellers. Whatever I say won't make them change their mind. In their eyes we're tinkers, thieves and murderers. Why on earth should they do anything to make our lives easier?'

'Murderers? Surely not?' Myra was shocked. 'I mean prejudice runs deep, but surely no one has ever accused your community of that crime?'

People were drifting back into the

room, taking their seats and shuffling their agendas.

'Debbie Astley, 1962? You ever heard of her, Detective Constable? And the young man who was hanged for her murder, though there was never a single shred of evidence to say that he was responsible?'

'I — no.'

She was certain she hadn't. She had only been nine in 1962. It was a long time ago. And yet that name, Debbie Astley, seemed so familiar.

'Look,' she said, resting her hand on his arm for a moment, 'we can't speak now. But after the meeting, right?'

★ ★ ★

Even now, almost a fortnight later, she was still wondering what had prompted her to suggest they should speak again once the meeting had broken up. Partly it was to do with Joseph Keogh himself. There was something dignified and noble about him, and she got the impression he was a person of great depth.

Throughout the remainder of the

meeting that name, Debbie Astley, had kept on running around her head. The feeling even continued while she was on her feet on the receiving end of hostile questioning, from Stuart Weeks and Bill Rigg among others, about what they described as the police's complete indifference to petty crime — a tarring and feathering she thought she dealt with competently, as it went.

Over a drink in the bar of the hotel opposite the Town Hall, Joseph Keogh filled Myra in on the details of the story he'd started to tell her. Debbie Astley, a sixteen-year-old, had been found dead, strangled with her own scarf. She'd been making her way home from the fair at the time of her attack. Witnesses claimed to have seen her talking and laughing with Sean Keogh, one of the travellers and a cousin of sorts to Joseph, who operated the fairground waltzer.

'He was a dead man walking, Detective Constable,' Joseph Keogh had said. 'I went to see him in prison before he was hanged. He swore that he'd never laid a finger on Debbie, and I believed him. But that was how it was in those days. He was a traveller. He'd been spotted talking to the girl. *Ergo* he'd killed her.'

There'd been no malice in Joseph Keogh's voice as he gave his account, only a trace of sadness. The story had stirred something within Myra and, since that evening, she'd dug out everything she could to do with the Astley case.

In fact, it was becoming an obsession with her, all the more so after the information her father had revealed when, on a visit to him at Cedarwood Hall, she'd asked him if he himself remembered anything.

He was surprised she couldn't bring Debbie to mind, he said. She used to babysit Myra occasionally. Had quite a thriving business babysitting for the entire street, as a matter of fact. He believed he had a photo of her somewhere — he'd dig it out for the next time Myra came round.

'Everybody loved her,' he said, his face sad. 'When they heard about her murder, the whole neighbourhood went into shock.'

Why wasn't Myra able to remember

anything about the murder? she asked her father. Surely it would have been the talk of the neighbourhood for months afterwards?

'We protected you from it,' he said. 'Didn't want to scare you — make you think you weren't safe any longer. I think maybe that was the way most of the parents went about it.'

The next time she dropped by, her father had found half a dozen photos of Debbie, always in among a group of smaller children, grinning at the camera or posing, glamour model-fashion, the belt of her coat pulled tight to emphasise a tiny waist.

'She was quite a looker,' Myra said.

Her dad agreed. He remembered taking these photos. Debbie always wanted to be there, at the forefront, he said. But she was no hussy, he added quickly, in case he gave Myra a bad impression of her.

'I'm sure she wasn't, Dad,' Myra said. 'But this lad, the one they hanged for it, do you really think he did it?'

'Without a doubt,' he said. 'There was

no reason to think otherwise.'

Myra wasn't so sure. Joseph had spoken about lack of evidence — had even suggested that vital evidence that would have proved his cousin innocent beyond doubt might have been destroyed. But there was no way of knowing. The only information that Myra had been able to get hold of had been from old newspapers. All the police reports and trial transcripts had long since been swallowed up by time and computerisation.

There was someone who might be able to help her out, though. Myra's colleague, PC Ed Willis, who fancied himself as a bit of a local historian, had promised that if she called in at the station en route to the party tonight, he might be able to supply her with the witness statements.

It was high time she wasn't here. She switched the radio off, silently cheering as Stuart Weeks' pontificating was swallowed up by the silence, and headed for the door.

Outside, the streets of Brising were surprisingly quiet, considering it was Saturday night. Frankly, Myra was relieved. It meant that no one could see her in this uniform. The material was heavy and scratchy. And how on earth did WPCs ever run in a straight skirt?

Ahead of her was the police station. Five minutes, that's all she needed, and then she'd be on her way. She ran up the steps and made her way inside.

But something wasn't quite right. In fact, nothing was. The furnishings were all wrong. The lighting, too. And what on earth had happened to the computers? Was that a typewriter on the desk? And she hadn't seen a phone like that since she was a little girl!

Someone — a sergeant, judging from his stripes — addressed her in a gruff voice.

'Oy, you! Get behind this desk. You're late. And there's a mound of filing to do.'

Dumbfounded, Myra stumbled towards the desk, glancing up at the walls as she did so, at the posters — all in black and white — that graced the walls. *Coughs and sneezes spread diseases,* she read. *Trap your germs in a handkerchief.* Next to it, someone had pinned up a calendar. The year said 1962.

2

Myra McAllister was proud to think that she was someone always able to hold her nerve. In all her years as a serving officer, she couldn't remember the last thing that had really fazed her. Not even her dad's stroke had come close. He was her dad, after all: indestructible, determined and as strong as an ox. Not for a minute had she believed he wouldn't pull through.

But this — well, this was scary. Where the heck was she, for one thing? It might say Brising Central Police Station on the plaque behind her head, just next to that gilt-edged portrait of a rather foxy-looking Queen Elizabeth, but it bore little resemblance to the Brising Central Police Station she'd walked out of yesterday evening at the end of another long shift — a paean to modern, green, technological efficiency.

Here, everything seemed topsy-turvy. There were huge radiators and tiny windows, and if she hadn't known it to be against the law to smoke in public buildings, she'd have sworn someone had been sneaking a crafty fag.

It was all very weird. Weirder still was her inability to work out *when* she was, let alone where. The calendar said 1962. How could that be possible? Yet she'd just been told to make tea for the sergeant before she helped WPC Morgan dust the filing cabinets. Which chimed pretty accurately with her knowledge of how women had been treated in the workplace back in those days.

'You can make tea, can't you?' the Sarge had barked, shooting her a look of such contempt that Myra was amazed she hadn't told him where to shove his tea bag and simply walked out.

'Yes, sir,' she'd replied instead.

Maybe if she'd been wearing the trousers she usually wore for work, instead of this hip-hugging skirt, she wouldn't have responded so obligingly.

She decided to think positively. Perhaps making tea could turn out to be a blessing in disguise. Running round her head, as she trailed through a warren of corridors to the kitchen, was the idea that very often, whenever she engaged in mundane tasks, complicated events had a habit of unravelling themselves. This time, however, the task left her just as baffled as before.

When WPC Carole Morgan found her in the kitchen, she was lost in thought, swishing a tea bag round and round in the one chip-free mug she'd located.

'Cancel the brew,' WPC Morgan said. 'There's been a shout. Which means there's only you and me and Derek on the premises, and I need you to help me man the desk.'

WPC Morgan looked glum.

'Cheer up,' Myra said. 'Gets us out of the dusting at least.'

'For now, maybe. But there's always dust.'

'There's always crime, too,' Myra pointed out.

'Yes, but none of it ever seems to come my way. I joined the police to see some action, not to teach schoolkids the Highway Code,' WPC Morgan complained. 'But every time something exciting comes up, it's the men who get to deal with it. It's not fair!'

Myra dropped the tea bag into the bin. That feeling of dislocation that had seized hold of her as soon as she'd walked into the building earlier seemed to have shaken her loose at last. She found herself suddenly gripped by curiosity.

'What exactly is it we're missing out on?'

'Only a murder,' Carole said. 'I've been listening in on the radio. Body of a young girl. Strangled near the fairground.'

Myra stiffened. 'Any ID?' she asked.

'Her library card identifies her as Debbie Astley.'

Myra felt the room tilt: 'Deep breaths, girl,' she told herself, 'and focus.' Now she knew exactly where she was. November 15th, 1962.

'Well, what on earth are we doing here then?' she said. 'Let's get down to the crime scene.'

She barged past Carole, who scurried behind, protesting that they couldn't possibly leave the station and reminding

Myra of the severity of the punishment that awaited them if they did.

'Look, Carole.' Myra grabbed an overcoat that looked like it might fit and slipped it on. 'You can't have it both ways. Either you're dusting or you're solving a murder. Which is it to be?'

A young PC with floppy hair and a scrubbed face was trying to look busy at the desk. Carole looked to be dithering at first. But then her face cleared.

'PC Stubbs,' she said. 'We've been called out. That means you're in charge.'

Stubbs looked up, flustered. 'What? Me?' he stammered.

'You'll be brilliant!' Myra said. 'You're a man, aren't you?'

She couldn't understand why her words seemed to cause Carole so much mirth.

* * *

In the alleyway where the body of sixteen-year-old Debbie Astley had been discovered by a courting couple, the tramp of human traffic was overwhelming. Myra groaned with dismay as uniformed and non-uniformed officers strode back and forth importantly, grinding their cigarette butts beneath their size-ten boots, seemingly unaware that they could well be destroying vital evidence.

'Who's running this operation?' she wondered aloud.

'CID, I suppose. With a helping hand from Sergeant Lowe over there, naturally. See him?'

Carole pointed out the bustling uniformed figure of the man who'd earlier instructed Myra to make him his tea. Lit up by the arc lights, he seemed to bristle with self-importance as he barked instructions to more menial members of the team, all of whom jumped at the sound of his voice. Something must have made him look in their direction, because suddenly there he was, striding over towards them.

'Oh-oh.' Carole shrank back into the darkness. 'Now we're for it.'

'Nonsense,' Myra boomed.

But her confidence drained away once she remembered she was in the uniform of a WPC and therefore Sergeant Lowe's inferior. Not that rank mattered much to a man like him, she guessed. She was already damned as his inferior by her gender.

'What are you two doing here?' he barked.

He glared at Myra, his tobacco-stained moustache twitching furiously. She sensed Carole trembling behind her and was determined to square up to him. No bully had ever got the better of her and they never would.

'We got a call,' she lied. 'CID. Thought the witnesses might need comforting.'

'That's right, sir,' Carole squeaked nervously.

'In that case you'd better get on with it,' he bawled.

The two women scrambled off in the direction he'd pointed them, to where a teenage couple, arms wrapped around each other for mutual comfort, stood lost and scared and somewhat detached from the bustle going on around them.

They'd already told their tale to another police officer, the boy, James

Fenton, explained in a hesitant voice, but they were both more than happy to repeat it. Myra guessed they'd be repeating it a few more times before the night ended and prayed that in the retelling they'd work the worst of their dreadful experience out of their systems.

Between them, each occasionally correcting or supporting what the other said, they told Myra they'd been on their way home from the fair. It was the girl — Sandy — who'd spotted the outline of the body first.

'We'd stopped for a moment, over by the wall there,' she said shyly, averting her eyes from Myra, whom she doubtless imagined had never had a boyfriend, so wouldn't be able to guess the reason why they'd broken their journey. 'She was there, next to the dustbin, where she still is.'

'Did you see or hear anyone running away?' Carole asked, looking from one to the other.

The girl glanced at her boyfriend, her eyes full of fear. Obviously she hadn't given it a thought till now that they might have been in the presence of the murderer.

'No,' they said, simultaneously.

'And did you approach her at all?' Myra wanted to know. 'It's important that if you've left any traces of your DNA on her coat, for instance, that we don't confuse it with the killer's.'

'DNA?'

Three pairs of puzzled eyes fixed themselves on her face. Myra realised what she'd said. She had no idea when exactly the police had started to rely on DNA in police work, but it certainly wasn't forty-six years ago.

'Fingerprints,' she said, correcting herself.

'Of course,' the boy said. 'I found this. Untied it from round her neck. Thought she might be still alive and I might be able to save her.'

He held out a dark blue paisley scarf. Myra gasped.

'I'm sorry,' he said. 'I should have given it straight to the officer but with everything going on it went right out of my mind.'

'Well, it'll be useless now,' Carole said, despairingly. 'If the murderer was foolish enough not to wear gloves when he strangled her then all his fingerprints will be overlaid with yours.'

'Not necessarily,' Myra said, and took the scarf carefully from the boy in her own gloved hands. 'If there's a trace of blood or hair or fibres from the murderer's clothes there's every chance we'll find him one day,' she said.

She was aware of Carole looking at her strangely, but chose to ignore it. Right now all she wanted was to get this item labelled and safely stored away, so that she could move on to something even more important which was to get as close as she could to the man in charge and find out everything he knew.

*   *   *

Carole was painting her toenails baby pink. It was easy to forget you were a woman, in this job, she told Myra with a sigh. Myra, dressed in a pair of ludicrously unflattering borrowed baby-doll pyjamas, having managed to fob Carole off with a story involving a chain of mishaps that started with a long-distance coach that broke down and ended with a mix-up with the luggage, didn't agree. If you were unlucky enough to have landed in Brising Central nick in 1962, like she apparently had, then being a woman was pretty much the only thing that defined you, and you were never going to be allowed to forget it.

It was being a woman that had landed her, along with Carole, the job of delivering James Fenton and his girlfriend, Sandy, back to their homes while their male equivalents in rank got to stay at the crime scene. 'Don't bother coming back,' they were told before setting off. 'There's nothing you're needed for back here, girls.'

'Except to make the tea,' Carole had muttered mutinously as they'd led the young couple away. Afterwards, she'd suggested Myra came back to stay with her at her mother's, upon hearing Myra — frantically crossing her fingers behind her back as she spoke — explain that she thought her landlady's husband had designs on her. A word to her mother and it was settled. Myra could stay as long as she liked.

Myra, tucked up in bed now, preferred not to think how long that would be. All she wanted to do was sleep and wake up in her own familiar bed. Carole's voice jolted her awake just as she felt herself drift off.

'That DNA thing you were talking about earlier. What is that?' she said.

Myra wriggled beneath the bed covers.

'Just something I picked up on a forensics course,' she hedged. 'They reckon one day in the future scientists will be able to work out what makes one human being different from another simply from a strand of hair or a speck of blood, or even a fingernail.'

'Really?' Carole, suddenly animated, snapped the light back on. 'So, if they find one single hair or some skin belonging to the murderer on that scarf, they'll know who it belongs to?'

'Yes, if he's on the database.' The words were out before Myra could check them.

'Database? What's that?'

'You know what, Carole? It's been a

long day. I'm shattered. And anyway, it was a short course. I don't remember much.'

'Forensic science, though. That's what I'd like to do some day. Though I expect they won't let me. It's mostly the men that do all that stuff.'

'You'll get there one day,' Myra said, with a yawn. 'Just keep pushing.'

'D'you really think so?'

Carole's tone was wistful, though Myra failed to hear it. She was fast asleep.

* * *

Myra was in Sergeant Lowe's bad books. So when he allocated her the task of visiting a couple of nice young men from good homes who'd been set upon by a bunch of pikeys in the pub, she refrained from asking him what had happened to police neutrality and the idea of being innocent until proven guilty.

The subject of prejudice had already come up between them when Sean Keogh was brought in and charged with the murder of Debbie Astley, just hours after her body had been found, and it was a conversation that had ended badly for Myra.

In fact, she'd been warned that one more act of insubordination would most certainly lead to a disciplinary charge. Myra didn't fancy that at all. She wanted to stay to the bitter end and uncover who Debbie's murderer really was. Because, as she'd said to Sergeant Lowe, she just didn't believe that Keogh was guilty. Where was the evidence, for one thing?

'You don't need no evidence, when your man confesses,' Lowe said, his bulbous eyes practically popping out at this challenge from a mere WPC.

'He's not even got a solicitor in there with him,' Myra said. 'The poor boy's probably been terrorised. He'd say anything.'

'I hope you're not accusing the police of bully-boy tactics, WPC McAllister!'

From the brief glimpse she'd had of Keogh, he'd looked lost and confused when he'd been brought in, whereas the two CID officers who'd accompanied him looked delighted at the prospect of the interrogation that lay ahead.

'Of course not,' she muttered.

'We've got witnesses who saw Keogh on the waltzer, laughing and flirting with the victim,' Lowe said, his smug tone suggesting that on this evidence alone the case was all sewn up.

'And then she left, didn't she? And he didn't.'

Myra had read all the witness statements. There was nothing written down that said he'd left his post and followed her.

'Just because nobody noticed him go, don't mean it never happened,' Lowe said. 'Devious lot they are. It's a well-known fact.'

She stood there smarting with fury while Lowe gave her the benefit of his theory. That Keogh had followed Debbie, because he thought he was on some sort of promise, but that she'd rejected him.

'That's when he lost control,' Lowe said. 'Animals. The lot of them.'

'You can't condemn a man because of some ridiculous prejudice against the race of people he belongs to!' Myra could contain her rage no longer. 'Only an idiot would think that.'

That's when Sergeant Lowe had put her on a warning. Now, in silence, she wrote down the addresses of both Stuart Weeks and Peter Burton and, in answer to Lowe's enquiry as to whether or not she knew that part of town, meekly replied that she did.

It was Stuart Weeks's mother who answered the door to Myra. She was a thin, nervous woman who kept up a constant stream of chatter as she led Myra into her best room, as she called it.

While they waited for Stuart to come down the stairs, Myra did her best to piece together the details of the attack from Mrs Weeks. The boys had been having a quiet drink in their local, she said. Stuart had come home from university for the weekend — Myra guessed Mrs Weeks managed to bring the fact that her son was studying for a law degree at Cambridge into every conversation — and he and Peter, an old school chum, had had a lot of catching up to do.

'Minding their own business, they

were. Next thing, they were set upon. Fairground lads. When they're not robbing people, they're beating them up or raping and killing our girls.'

'Mum!'

Neither of them had heard Stuart, shod in slippers, come downstairs and slip into the room. He held out his hand politely and apologised for his mother's outburst.

'She worries about me,' he said. 'You know what mums are like.'

Obviously, the effects of his one term as an undergraduate at one of England's finest universities had already rubbed off on him. There was no trace of a local accent and his manners, as she'd just witnessed for herself, were impeccable.

'It's not nice for mums to see their sons battered and bruised,' she conceded.

He put up a hand to his face and gave a modest grin.

'If you don't mind, Mrs Weeks,' Myra said, 'I'd like to speak to Stuart alone.'

Mrs Weeks scurried off with a polite 'of course', but it was obvious she felt peeved at being excluded. Stuart seemed to relax once his mother had gone. Myra didn't blame him. Doting mothers must be such an embarrassment to a young man, she mused.

Stuart backed up his mother's story. Neither of them had noticed the men at the bar. They'd been too busy talking, he said. And frankly, his memory was hazy. Maybe he stepped back on someone's toe or nudged a drop of beer from his attacker's glass. Whatever it was that had provoked the incident, it was over now. He wouldn't have reported it at all had his mother not insisted.

'Like I said, Officer. She worries about me,' he said.

'Your mother says they were fairground boys.'

He agreed they might have been. He certainly didn't know any of them, if that was what she was thinking. When she asked if his friend had been attacked, too, Stuart said that Peter had appeared to get away scot-free.

'Why do you think that was?'

Stuart shrugged. He'd no idea, he said defensively. And since he had no intentions of bringing charges, it really didn't matter. At that, he offered to show her to the door. Their interview was clearly at an end.

Why had he seemed so anxious to get rid of her? Myra wondered. Was he afraid that these boys might come after him again if he pressed charges? Something about the way he'd reacted when she'd asked him why he thought he'd been the one targeted and not his friend intrigued her. He was obviously intelligent enough to realise that her question wasn't a frivolous one. Well, he was right about that.

Peter Burton was bruise-free, just as Stuart had said. Plump, with a pronounced local accent, he had none of his best chum's confidence, and Myra liked him for it. It seemed natural to her that, faced with the law, Peter should be nervous. What was unnatural was Stuart's supreme self-assurance. It was as if he'd spent all morning rehearsing his answers.

Peter, on the contrary, muddled up the answers to the questions Myra fired at him. How long had the two boys known each other? Since primary school; no, they'd first met at cubs. What was Stuart doing home in the middle of term? Something to do with his mother, or was it an uncle? Did he often come? Not sure. He'd been twice already. Or maybe three or four times, now he thought about it. Did he have a girlfriend here? No, he didn't. Not as far as Peter knew. Strange answer, didn't he think? They were best friends, weren't they? Surely Stuart would have mentioned a girlfriend, if one had existed? With each mumbled reply, Peter grew more and more flustered.

'Why would Stuart allow this crime of assault to go unchallenged, Peter? Just days after a man from the same travelling community has been charged with the murder of Debbie Astley? You'd think he'd want to do his bit to restore order to the town, wouldn't you? Him studying law and all?'

'I — I really don't know, Officer,' Peter said. 'You'll have to ask him that.'

'Maybe I will, Peter,' she said.

At the door, just when, she guessed, he thought he was rid of her at last, she asked him if he'd known Debbie.

'She went to the girls' grammar just next to your school, didn't she?' she said.

'Did she? I didn't know that, Officer.'

Another lie, she was certain. But why? And who was he protecting? His best friend? Or himself?

Back at the station, she heard Sergeant Lowe's thunderous voice before she saw him. He loomed large behind the desk, his face red and his moustache twitching terrifyingly.

'You!' he yelled.

Myra was already over the threshold. All eyes were on her. In particular, those of a baffled-looking WPC still in her overcoat, who hovered by the desk, occasionally glancing at Lowe for guidance.

'This young woman has turned up to start her tour of duty at Brising Central,' he said, drawing out the words.

The WPC smiled nervously.

'When I told her there must have been some sort of mistake because we already had our new WPC, she presented me with this letter.'

He flapped the letter in Myra's face.

Myra, meanwhile, prayed for deliverance. It came in the shape of WPC Carole Morgan, carrying a tray of tea. From the worried look she gave Myra, she was obviously aware of the situation. Maybe she'd even volunteered — for once — to make the tea, so that she could give herself time to work out how best she could help Myra. Because Myra didn't have a clue how she was going to help herself.

Lowe slapped the letter down on the desk and began to make his way from behind it.

'You are an imposter!' he yelled.

He reached out to make a grab for her just as Carole stepped between them and let slip the tea tray. Lowe yelled, Carole squealed, and Myra made a dash for it down the steps, along the street and round the corner, without a glance behind her and only stopping when she reached Brising Town Square.

The windows of the Guildhall were flooded with light. Myra heard music playing and the sound of revellers having a good time. Exhausted and out of breath, she crept up the steps and pushed open the door.

This way to the Sixties Police Charity Disco, read the sign in the grand entrance hall. Ann Harris, her modern-day colleague, dressed in miniskirt and white boots, was behind the desk, collecting tickets.

'Glad you could make it, Myra,' she said. 'Come on in!'

3

Too many daytime hours spent scanning old newspaper articles on microfiche, and sleepless nights in which she attempted to piece everything together, had left Myra with an incipient headache and a bad case of dry eyes.

Much of what she'd discovered about Stuart Weeks, Brising's MP since 1992, was new to her. Initially, he'd been voted in on a tidal wave of support. Subsequent elections had shrunk his majority, but if he was less popular now than previously, he was still a local boy. And this counted a great deal with an electorate automatically suspicious of anybody who wasn't native born and bred.

On the surface, Myra learned, he'd led a blameless life. Brought up by a hard-working single mother, he'd won a scholarship to Cambridge. From there, he'd joined the Home Office as a policy adviser before swapping his role behind

223

the scenes for one centre stage.

Along the way he'd managed to collect an attractive, well-connected wife, Julia, with whom he'd spawned two children. With his appointment as a junior minister in the new cabinet, it must have seemed to Stuart Weeks that life was sweet.

Then disaster arrived, in the shape of Diana Palmuir. Myra had only a vague memory of the scandal, so the screeching headlines and excessive speculation of the newspapers — both broadsheets and tabloids — proved gripping reading.

There was never any suggestion of foul play the morning that Diana Palmuir, Weeks' secretary, was discovered in her bed, dead from an overdose. But what began as a trickle of suggestion that there was more to Weeks' relationship with the attractive twenty-four-year-old very quickly grew into a tidal wave of rumour and assertion.

Weeks denied it, insisting their relationship had never been anything other than totally professional. Like a true political wife, Julia stood by him, smiling stoically at the camera — (not at her husband,

Myra noticed) — in the driveway of their smart house, the children standing supportively by.

In the way of all political scandals, the story died down after a while. Myra guessed that Weeks must have been kept out of the party limelight deliberately after that, to give people time to forget. Then, gradually, his name began to pop up again. One clipping in particular caught her eye, in which he expressed his sorrow at the death of his great political ally, Fred Crook — burned to death in a fire at his office — and, for the first time, Myra saw him as a man with tender feelings.

She just wished there was someone at work she could talk to about all this. It was a burden she carried round with her, a certainty that Sean Keogh had had nothing to do with the murder of Debbie Astley.

But who would be interested enough to listen to her suspicions? And how could she convince them that something wasn't right? This crime had been committed more than forty years previously and, according to the law, justice had been carried out. There was no reason at all to revisit the circumstances of Debbie's death.

Besides, she could hardly tell people that she'd been present at the original crime scene — had witnessed, in fact, the whole area being treated with such little care that any real evidence was bound to have been either destroyed or too badly sullied to be of any use.

In the end, she found herself discussing the case with her dad when she went to see him — though in truth it was she who did all the talking while he just listened and nodded at appropriate points, occasionally, like now, throwing in a pertinent question.

'So what is it you've got against this Stuart Weeks, then? Apart from the fact that he's a politician?'

They were sitting in the corner of the day room at Cedarwood Hall, as far away from the TV as Mr McAllister felt comfortable with. Occasionally, he would turn his head in that direction, pretending he wasn't really interested in what was going on in Albert Square. But Myra guessed that *EastEnders* held far more fascination for him than her own inconsequential wittering. Hardly surprising really, since she'd bored him to sleep with it every night this week.

'I wish I could tell you, Dad,' she said sadly.

And she really did wish she could. Tell him that Stuart Weeks had been as shifty as a young man as he was as an older one.

There was something else she could do, though. Peter Burton had been harder to find than Weeks, being a man who'd always kept himself out of the public eye. But Myra wasn't a detective for nothing and she'd found him in the end. And tomorrow, her day off, she was going to pay him a little visit. They had some catching up to do.

★ ★ ★

As she drove down the muddy track that led to the large, tumbledown building and barns that comprised Satis Farm, Myra wondered what had led Peter Burton to decide to throw in his well-paid job in town planning and open a commune in the middle of the countryside for eco-warriors like himself. Had he been running away from something? She wondered.

The Eighties-inspired obsession with materialism, for sure — *Satis* meant 'enough' in Latin, she'd learned — and, on a sunny, mild day like today, with the farm dogs teasing each other playfully in the yard, the faint bleat of sheep coming from the nearby hills and the noise of traffic only noticeable by its absence, she could imagine living here would be more than enough for anyone. But what if Burton had fled to this place for deeper, more sinister reasons? Well, she mused, as Burton himself strode towards her, this was what she was here to discover.

As she remembered him, Peter Burton had been a plump, spotty boy with a pronounced local accent, painfully shy and unable to look her in the eye. These days, he was much thinner, skinny even, but just as stiff in his manner. He greeted

Myra pleasantly enough — all trace of his former accent removed — and led her inside. He'd been expecting her, he said, and had made a batch of scones in her honour.

'You must wonder why I want to speak to you,' she said.

'Not at all,' he said. 'My conscience is clear. The nearest I've ever come to a brush with the law is having a girlfriend at Greenham Common.'

They used to have a great many police visits in the past, he added, generally to do with the law's suspicion that any group of people who chose to set up a commune in the middle of nowhere were either growing cannabis or into Satanic practices.

'Tell me about Stuart Weeks, Mr Burton.'

The change in Peter Burton was swift. Once again he was the hesitant, nervous, stumbling boy she'd first met in that other Brising.

'What can I tell you about Stuart that isn't already in the public domain, Inspector?'

Setting down on the table a plate of well-risen scones that would have shamed Nigella Lawson, he sat down awkwardly. Myra's mouth was watering, but now was not the time to change the subject with requests to pass the jam and butter.

It was the stuff that wasn't in the public domain that interested her, she said. How would Peter describe their friendship, for example? Peter's guard was up now, for sure, Myra could see.

'OK,' he said. 'You've obviously got an agenda here, so I won't waste any of your time by trying to sidetrack you.'

Myra said she was glad to hear it and, when he hesitated, prompted him with her own words.

'You two were best friends, no?'

'When it was convenient for Stuart. He liked girls, and they liked him. Which meant that, more often than not, I got dropped in favour of one of the fairer sex.'

He spoke entirely without malice, almost as if he was poking fun at his younger self. Once more, Myra felt herself drawn to him.

'Are you gay, Mr Burton? Is that what you're saying?'

He shook his head. 'No,' he said. 'Although I must admit that my feelings for Stuart — frighteningly intense in those days — convinced me I was at one time. I admired his brilliance and his confidence when we were teenagers, that's all, and I wanted to be like him.'

'Debbie Astley. Where did she fit in?'

'Debbie? Why are you asking me about her?'

He placed his hands on the table. They were knotted with veins and bore the scars of a man who worked on the land. He bit his nails, she noticed. From his next question it became apparent that while she'd been studying his hands, he'd been studying her face.

'I can't help feeling I've met you before,' he said. 'But for the life of me I can't remember when.'

'Memory's like that,' Myra said, inwardly flinching. 'What's your memory like about the weekend Debbie Astley was murdered?'

'Debbie was one of a string of

girlfriends for Stuart,' he said. 'She was sweet. Too good for him. That weekend he'd come home to tell her it was over. He'd met somebody else at Cambridge — somebody better, he said — a judge's daughter.'

'Julia,' Myra said.

He nodded. 'He'd come round to my place to tell me he planned to let her know that night. At the fair.'

There was a brief pause, heavy with meaning, before Myra spoke again.

'You spoke to a police officer about an assault on Weeks in a pub, remember?'

'They asked me if I could think of a reason why Stuart had been assaulted and I said no, I couldn't.'

'That's right.'

'Only I lied, because I was starting to put two and two together. The young men who'd gone after Stuart were related to the boy who'd been charged with Debbie's murder,' he said. 'I think Stuart was convinced they'd have killed him if the landlord hadn't called the police so quickly. I overheard one of them muttering that Stuart should watch his back.'

Once his wounds had healed, Peter said, Stuart had fled back to the safety of his Cambridge college. From that time, he stopped spending vacations in Brising completely.

'It played on my mind that Stuart had told me he was going to meet Debbie that night,' Peter went on. 'So much so that I felt the need to pay a call at the police station and report it,' he said. 'I felt awful. Some kid was about to go on trial for Debbie's murder and there was I, withholding evidence.'

'What happened there?'

'I spoke to someone. They said they'd look into it and that was that. I thought I was bound to get a visit later and be asked to make a statement, but no, nothing.'

'I don't suppose you remember who you spoke to?'

'A man. Old. Old to me, anyway. I was a kid back then. I remember he was a sergeant. At one time, I fancied myself in uniform and I knew all the ranks.'

'Sgt Lowe,' Myra thought. Without a doubt. Just when he thought he'd got one of the travellers banged to rights — the people he hated most in the whole of Brising — some cocky young lad had to turn up and put a spanner in the works. Hardly surprising that he brushed this new evidence under the carpet.

'When nothing happened, and that boy was hanged, I felt bad for a time, but then, well, you know what it's like, Inspector.'

She nodded. 'Life gets in the way,' she said.

'But then another couple of things happened that made me think about Stuart again. That secretary. He was cleared of any involvement with her. But I'd seen Stuart around girls. How he could manipulate them and break their hearts. If she killed herself, you can bet Stuart would have driven her to it.'

'And the other thing, Peter?'

Peter clenched and unclenched his fists.

'That fire. Someone died. But it was no accident.'

★ ★ ★

234

A fortnight had passed since Myra's visit to Peter Burton, during which time she'd slept better than she'd done in ages, due to the fact that she was no longer running this case single-handedly and in her time off. Other departments were involved now, leaving her time to think about how best to approach Weeks.

She'd been thinking of others, too. Of poor Sean Keogh, whose life had been snatched from him through prejudice and ignorance. And of Debbie Astley. The night she died, she'd been babysitting Myra, so her father had informed her. She was in trouble with them, because she'd left the nine-year-old Myra on her own in front of the TV and slipped off early.

'You told us she had a date. That she had something very important to tell her boyfriend and that it was a coincidence because he'd said he had something equally important to tell her.'

He'd made a joke of it, said they should have known even then that, with her memory for flawless recollection of the facts, Myra was destined for the police service. Myra, apparently, had attempted to defend Debbie. She wouldn't have gone unless it had been urgent, she said, and Mummy and Daddy must promise not to go round in the morning and tell Debbie off. In the event, they never did, of course.

Now, as Myra rang the doorbell of Stuart Weeks' palatial residence, she did her best to push Debbie to the back of her mind. Too many times, recently, she'd imagined her applying her lipstick in the brown-spotted mirror in Myra's front room, buzzing with anticipation about what, exactly, Stuart wanted to tell her. All the way there, she must have been hoping it was that he loved her and then she'd be able to tell him about the baby.

Maybe he hadn't been there at the fair, in the place where he'd said he'd be, and she'd treated herself to a ride on the waltzer where, in full view of dozens of witnesses, she'd bantered with Sean Keogh. Maybe she'd checked her watch after a couple of spins, and concluded he'd had enough time to get to their rendezvous by now. She'd waved goodbye to Sean and strolled away. To meet her death.

*   *   *

Stuart Weeks' wife, Julia, was elegant, fragrant and cold. She showed not the slightest interest in knowing what it was Myra wanted with her husband, but simply rustled off to another part of the house once she'd called him from his study, leaving a trail of expensive perfume behind her.

Weeks bustled in, rubbing his hands together in a hail-fellow-well-met imitation of a man suggesting the day was chilly. Although the facts that the temperature in his well-appointed drawing room was probably hovering around the seventy-eight-degree mark and he was in his shirtsleeves made rather a mockery of his charade.

He thrust out his hand in welcome. Myra declined it.

'This isn't a social visit, Mr Weeks,' she said. 'I'm here to talk to you about the deaths of Debbie Astley and Fred Crook.'

He looked first puzzled, then indignant. What on earth were the police doing wasting their resources going over old crimes long solved, he demanded, when there were so many unsolved crimes that they'd still got nowhere with?

'On the contrary, Mr Weeks,' Myra said. 'New evidence in both these cases has led us to reopen our enquiries.'

Stuart Weeks' face was a picture of deadpan immobility. What was he thinking? Myra wondered. That he could still bluff it out, or that the time had arrived for him to call his doubtless very expensive solicitor?

'I went to see an old friend of yours recently,' Myra said. 'I'm sure you remember Peter Burton?'

Weeks tilted his head slightly to show he did.

'Did you know that he runs a commune now? Quite successfully, actually. Dabbles in organic produce, plays around with solar power and all that stuff. Makes a mean scone, too.'

Myra was enjoying herself, though she knew she shouldn't be.

'Very nice, I'm sure,' Weeks said, puzzled.

'The weekend Debbie Astley died . . . I do beg your pardon. I should correct myself — was murdered.'

During Myra's preamble, Weeks had perched himself on the fat arm of a plush, red velvet settee, so that now she was looking down on him.

'Peter tells me that, for years, he's had rather a bad conscience about his behaviour around that time.'

'Oh? Why's that?'

'Something about his loyalty to you getting in the way of the truth. And how he'd omitted to mention, when asked, that you'd told him how you'd planned to meet Debbie at the fair that night, to tell her you'd got another girlfriend and the two of you were finished.'

Weeks relaxed, slid on to the settee proper, and smiled up at Myra.

'I do wish you'd sit down,' he said. 'You're making me feel nervous.'

Except she knew the opposite was the case. They both knew that whatever Peter Burton had said was just words. And just words would convict no one. He may have *said* that, Weeks said, but in the event he hadn't followed it through.

'I was a coward. I should have gone to the fair that night and done the honest thing by Debbie. Instead of which, I let her draw her own conclusion.'

'You were a young man, Mr Weeks. Young men can behave very shabbily to young women and that's a fact.'

For a moment, she held Weeks' eyes, taunting him to remember that other young girl he'd treated so badly that she'd ended up committing suicide.

'Oh,' she said, 'I didn't tell you, did I, what else your old friend gets up to in that commune of his. He takes in waifs and strays.'

'Cats and dogs, you mean?'

'Well, not exactly. More people down on their luck. Men who've turned to crime to support a habit, then whose conscience gets the better of them. He gives them a home. Doesn't ask questions. But after a while, once they've started to feel they can trust him, they begin to open up.'

Weeks was sitting bolt upright, hugging his knees. He didn't try to interrupt when Myra brought up the name of Jonty Clayton, party member and party animal, who, for a regular supply of cocaine, had willingly set the fire in the offices of the man who, according to Jonty, who had it from the horse's mouth — the horse in question being his boss, Stuart Weeks — was in possession of numerous love letters that had passed between Weeks and Diana Palmuir. Letters that proved, beyond doubt, that their relationship went far beyond the professional, suggesting, as they did, that Weeks intended ending his marriage for her.

'The Press would have had a field day with that one, eh, Mr Weeks? Not to mention your wife. This house in her name, is it? Like the French chalet.'

Weeks began a furious protest, jerking his arms and legs like a puppet on knotted string. Who would believe anything that a self-confessed addict said? he demanded. He'd had enough of these ridiculous claims, and unless she had any real proof then Myra should leave immediately and never darken his door again. A series of harsh rings on the front doorbell brought his tirade to an end.

'Oh,' Myra said. 'That'll be my colleagues. And you needn't worry about Jonty Clayton. You're quite right, the coke got the better of him in the end. It was probably a load of nonsense, anyway.'

Weeks visibly relaxed. When his wife put her head round the door to introduce PCs Clarke and Thompson, he beamed affably.

'You've got an escort,' he said.

'On the contrary, Mr Weeks,' Myra said, beaming back. '*You* have.'

★　★　★

It had been proved beyond a shadow of a doubt that the speck of blood on the scarf that had strangled Debbie Astley was Stuart Weeks'. Of course, Myra mused, making her way over to Joseph Keogh's, it had been Weeks' own fault that he'd got caught.

If he hadn't felt the need to take a

stand against the 'woolly-minded liberals who were convinced that DNA profiling betokened the end of the individual's right to privacy', he'd never have put himself forward for the publicity stunt of allowing his own DNA to be taken as proof that the system had his complete backing.

And if WPC Carole Morgan hadn't had such faith in Myra back in 1962 and gone along with her assertion that one day in the future a murderer could well be convicted from as little evidence as a hair, she wouldn't have taken such pains to ensure that the scarf used to strangle Debbie had been properly bagged up and handed over directly to the man in charge of forensics, bypassing her Sergeant. Myra was convinced that he'd very likely have destroyed it in case it was ever proved to bear the traces of someone other than the man he intended fitting up for Debbie's death.

Sean Keogh, of course, sentenced to his own dreadful death, had been just as much a victim as poor Debbie Astley. But whereas Debbie had been mourned and her reputation left unsullied, Sean had only ever been lamented by his own community. A community that for ever after had been tainted by association.

Now was the time to put that right. This afternoon, the townsfolk of Brising, alongside members of the travelling community, various bigwigs and representatives of the clergy and the police, had gathered on Old Moor to dedicate this plot of land — now a permanent site for any travellers who wished to stay here — to Sean Keogh.

Joseph Keogh brushed a tear away from his eye and held out his hand to Myra, who took it and gripped it tightly.

'Thank you, Myra,' he said, 'for all you've done to restore the good name of my kinsman and my community.'

'Please, Joseph. It wasn't all down to me. I got the ball rolling, that's all.'

'But we'll always bless you for it,' he said. 'In fact, you don't know it yet, but you're now an honorary member of the travelling community.'

Myra didn't know what to say. An honorary traveller. That was good. Then again, she was a bit of an expert on travelling, wasn't she? Although that was something she definitely intended keeping to herself.

THE END

Young heiress Cynthia Mason lives with her violent stepfather, Samuel Kimber, the controller of her fortune — until she marries. So when she becomes engaged to Peter Lorrimer, she fears Kimber's reaction. Peter, due to call and take her away, talks to Kimber in his study. Meanwhile, Cynthia has tiptoed downstairs and gone — she's vanished without trace. Her friend Miss Frayle, secretary to the criminologist Dr. Morelle, tries to find her — and finds herself a target for murder!

THE EVIL BELOW

Richard A. Lupoff

'*Investigator seeks secretary, amanuensis, and general assistant. Applicant must exhibit courage, strength, willingness to take risks and explore the unknown . . .* ' In 1905, John O'Leary had newly arrived in San Francisco. Looking for work, he had answered the advert, little understanding what was required for the post — he'd try anything once. In America he found a world of excitement and danger . . . and working for Abraham ben Zaccheus, San Francisco's most famous psychic detective, there was never a dull moment . . .

A STORM IN A TEACUP

Geraldine Ryan

In the first of four stories of mystery and intrigue, *A Storm in a Teacup*, Kerry has taken over the running of her aunt's café. After quitting her lousy job and equally lousy relationship with Craig, it seemed the perfect antidote. But her chef, with problems of his own, disrupts the smooth running of the café. Then, 'food inspectors' arrive, and vanish with the week's takings. But Kerry remembers something important about the voice of one of the bogus inspectors . . .

SÉANCE OF TERROR

Sydney J. Bounds

Chalmers decides to attend one of Dr. Lanson's nightly séances because it's somewhere warm to rest his weary feet. A decision he regrets when a luminous cloud forms above the assembled people. Strangely, from the cloud comes a warning: someone there is about to die to prevent them from revealing secrets. A man defiantly leaps to his feet, the lights are extinguished, the man's voice is cut off and an ear-piercing shriek reverberates around the room . . .